FUK SHYT

**Lock Down Publications &
Ca$h Presents**
FUK SHYT
By BLAKK DIAMOND

Fuk Shyt

Lock Down Publications
P.O. Box 870494
Mesquite, Tx 75187

Visit our website at **www.lockdownpublications.com**

Copyright 2019 Fuk Shyt

First Edition August 2019
Printed in the United States of America

This is a work of fiction. Names, characters, places, and incidents either are products of the author's imagination or are used fictitiously. Any similarity to actual events or locales or persons, living or dead, is entirely coincidental.

Cover design and layout by: Dynasty's Cover Me
Book interior design by: Shawn Walker

Stay Connected with Us!

Text **LOCKDOWN** to 22828 to stay up-to-date with new releases, sneak peaks, contests and more…

Thank you!

Submission Guideline.

Submit the first three chapters of your completed manuscript to ldpsubmissions@gmail.com, subject line: Your book's title. The manuscript must be in a .doc file and sent as an attachment. Document should be in Times New Roman, double spaced and in size 12 font. Also, provide your synopsis and full contact information. If sending multiple submissions, they must each be in a separate email.

Have a story but no way to send it electronically? You can still submit to LDP/Ca$h Presents. Send in the first three chapters, written or typed, of your completed manuscript to:

LDP: Submissions Dept
Po Box 870494
Mesquite, Tx 75187

DO NOT send original manuscript. Must be a duplicate.

Provide your synopsis and a cover letter containing your full contact information.

Thanks for considering LDP and Ca$h Presents.

Prologue

The two boys crept through the vacant house of a known drug dealer in the neighborhood, picking up valuable things such as games, jewelry, and other things that interested their young minds. This was the second house they had hit today, but the first house didn't produce anything but a bag full of condoms and sex movies. So, they decided to give their luck one more try and came to an agreement that they would hit the weed man they knew as Todd.

The taller dread-headed boy walked up the stairs slowly with his brother behind him until they got on the second level of the house.

The short dark-skinned boy pointed up, then said, "It sounds like somebody is in here, bruh."

The taller boy strained his ears and became aware of the sounds also.

"Look, go ahead and hit the rooms up. I'm about to go upstairs and see what the fuck going on," whispered the taller boy as he stared at his brother who was weighing the options in his head, not liking the part about splitting up now knowing there were other people in the house. Deciding wasn't hard, but the shorter boy knew they didn't have much time, so he responded, "Look, nigga, stay the fuck out the way. Just watch them folks and make sure they don't come down here."

The taller boy nodded then stuck his right arm out for a pound in which his brother pounded before they headed their separate ways. The tall boy took a step up the stairs that led to the third level of the house and then another one. The sounds became clearer and the tall boy heard sounds of a woman begging a man for more and grunts from a man. Stepping onto the third floor, the tall boy looked at the only

7

door on the third floor and saw that it was slightly cracked, then tip-toed to it. The sounds of a sexual escapade filled his ears and caused curiosity to take control of his mind. The tall boy got on his knees, put his head to the door and tried to look through the crack, but he couldn't see much, so he pushed the door as gently as he could, opening it just enough where he could stick his head in.

The tall boy flung his dreads out of his face, then tied a rubber band around them that he had on his right wrist and got back on his hands and knees. He then moved closer to the door and stuck his head slowly into the room, turning it to the sounds of the session.

"Ooh, baby, nigga get this pussy!" shouted a dark-skinned woman as a light-skinned man pump in her like a jackrabbit.

The tall boy had to stop himself from laughing at the sight of what had to be a 250-pound fat woman getting fucked by a skinny dude who looked like a pencil with his face screwed up in concentration. The tall boy looked around the room and spotted a big screen television playing music videos and a table with liquor bottles lining it and some other miscellaneous shit. The tall boy then turned his head toward another table in the room and spotted a bag of weed.

'Oh, shit I gotta get that!' thought the boy as he weighed his options. *'Fuck it,'* he thought looking at the man whose back was to him. The fat black woman was looking forward as the man fucked her from behind on the bed. The boy pushed the door open, dropped on his stomach and began crawling slowly on the floor.

'Oh, shit!' thought the boy as he came up on what looked like a pair of panties the size of a beach towel. The boy picked the panties up, then threw them to the side and

crawled a few more feet, reaching the table. The boy then grabbed the weed and what looked like a bag of X-pills off the table, then slowly made his way backward.

"Oh, bitch, I'm about to cum!" the man said.

The boy turned his head and saw the man pumping even more vigorously making the fat woman's ass move like Jell-O.

'Time to go,' thought the boy as he made it to the door and slipped through.

The boy then got to his feet, headed down the stairs silently, stepped on the second floor and walked into each room until he found his brother who was going through a closet.

"Bruh, I ain't no money or drugs," the short boy said as he turned and saw his brother entering the closet.

"Bruh, let's go. The folks coming and besides we straight," the taller boy stated holding up the weed and the x-pills.

"Baby, you got a nigga tired as fuck," a voice stated, that sounded nearer than it was supposed to.

"Oh, shit!" Both the boys said before they turned and ran out of the room taking the steps two at a time.

The man shouted, "I know ain't nobody in my fucking house! Melissa, get my shotgun!"

The two boys headed out the back door of the house into the woods with their stolen goods laughing uncontrollably at another close call.

Blakk Diamond

Chapter 1

The classroom was filled with noise as the students gossiped loudly amongst themselves about drugs, sex, guns, who's who, and who's not, oblivious to the teacher's presence. The class smelled of cigarette smoke, weed and a combination of perfumes that five girls wore.

It was May, the end of the school year, for Lorenzo 'Lo' Preston, it was his last day at the alternative school called, '*The Last Hope*.' Lo had gotten kicked out of public school for fighting in the 6th grade and was sent to the school with the worst of the bad kids in his age range. At first, he was timid and anti-social, but that died quickly as he became accustomed to the *'outlaw'* mentality everyone possessed at the school and even some of the teachers dealt with them as if they were at a street function.

Lo' sat back in his desk in a slouched position watching his latest girlfriend Miracle count his money, showcasing it in front of her friends who Lo had either gone with before her or secretly had sex with behind her back, but that was how it went.

Miracle had honey-brown skin, with the facial structure of a Nubian goddess, but with a more developed body that had all the young niggas trying to smash. Miracle, however, declined them knowing she had the best one now. Lo pulled his purple and black diamond fitted baseball cap further down his face, hiding his reddened eyes from the watermelon dro' he and his friend Carrot-Top had just finished smoking in the bathroom on the 7th-grade hall. Lo was already tipping from the blue dolphin pill he had split with his big brother Gerod who everybody called Rod in the high school part of the alternative school.

Lo and Rod had popped the pill earlier that day before they went their separate ways after breakfast. Lo, being that it was his first time popping a pill, was geeked out of his mind.

"Lo, you been tripping all day," Shaneka said who was a dark-skinned girl with hazel eyes and a slim petite frame from Cascade. Who Lo' had just fucked last week in the bathroom on the 6th grade hallway.

"Nah, I'm straight, I'm just on some mo' shit, right now," Lo replied as he lifted his cap off his long dreadlocks the color of coal and sat up in his desk looking Shaneka in the eyes intensely wanting her to know that he wanted her which caused Shenaka to smile slyly looking toward Miracle. Lo shrugged his shoulders letting Shaneka know that Miracle wouldn't stop nothing.

Ring! Ring! The bell sounded through the school letting everybody know school was over. Shaneka picked up her phone and held it indicating for Lo' to call before turning and giving Lo' a good view of her voluptuous frame. Lo' stared for a second before turning his intention to Miracle.

Miracle took twenty dollars out of the bankroll of money Lo had given her to flip through, then stood and kissed him deeply. After breaking the kiss, Miracle asked, "You gon' meet me at Skate Town?"

Lo nodded his head, too geeked to say anything as he stood. Lo pulled his blue button up shirt out of his beige khaki pants that everyone at the school had to wear and headed toward the door with the rest of the kids as they rushed to get to the parking lot to politic with friends before they left school.

Lo was stopped by Mr. McCoy, the teacher of the class he was walking out of. Mr. McCoy was a laid back, old school cat who stood 6'3 with a slim frame and a slight pudge from drinking. Mr. McCoy took off the glasses perched on his nose and said with emotion and roughness only a father would have for a son, "I know this is your last day at school and honestly I don't see how you made it through. Listen, you should plan for the future in order to be successful. Please don't do nothing stupid this summer. I want to see you make it son." Mr. McCoy had been Lo's teacher since 6th grade and had watched the young boy grow from a shy kid to a slick, conniving, womanizing criminal. It hurt him because he couldn't save him from the bad influences around him.

"I'ma be straight," said Lo as he hid his eyes behind his dreads.

Mr. McCoy grabbed his shoulder with his right hand and with his left he swept Lo's dreads out of his face, looked into his eyes and saw he was under the influence. Mr. McCoy only shook his head and said, "Go on, enjoy your summer and make sure you take heed to what I just said."

Nodding, Lo' pushed out of the class and turned left. He walked through an exit door that led to a spiral staircase, walked down the stairs and pushed open another door that led to the lobby of the building and went out the double doors leading to the parking lot of the school. As soon as Lo stepped into the parking lot he heard the sound of sound systems on full blast and smelled weed from the numerous blunts that were being passed around right in front of the resource officers who couldn't do shit about it because they would have to lock the whole school up and they didn't possess that type of manpower.

Lo' weaved through the crowded parking lot that looked like a car show convention as young niggas from the high school part of the school flexed their whips. All old school Cutlasses to Chevelles with bright colors and chrome wheels filled the lot as brash students came out of their shirts. Some threw them in the sky and watched them hit the ground while others tucked them in their backpacks and put on some regular street wear. Lo paid no attention to the calls from some of his partners, girls, and other people as he headed to the bus too geeked to be standing in the hot ass sun.

Lo stepped on the bus and greeted Ms. Jones who was a heavy-set woman, with blood curls cut down into a mini fro. Lo cut Ms. Jones grass from time to time and she paid him and baked him a cake. Ms. Jones was a loner, who lived by herself, so she enjoyed the company of Lo and his brother Rod. Lo walked past other students and took a seat at the back of the bus. Stephanie, who everybody called Step, was sitting in front of him by herself. Step was Lo's lil' freak, every day after school on their way to the house, Step gave Lo a hand job, something Lo looked forward to every day.

"Lorenzo, why you staring like that?" Step asked.

She had her long hair going down her back, was dark-skinned and very mature for her age. Who honestly was forced to grow up being that she had a little girl, plus a mother who used crack. Lo liked Step, shawty was a very down to earth person and he liked kicking it with her from time to time at basis and terms that there were not spoken on, but silently agreed upon.

"I'm good. Why everybody keep asking that? I feel good as a mu'fucka, dumb mellow," Lo said as he turned his head to the right and looked out the window into the parking lot, seeing confusion. Lo jumped up after spotting his brother Rod in the midst of the confusion.

"Lorenzo, sit down!" Ms. Jones shouted who had also spotted Rod and knew it would only be a matter of seconds before Lo spotted him.

Bucking on Ms. Jones, Lo turned to the exit door and opened it. Then jumped off the back of the bus with only one thing on his mind, helping his brother go up against whoever wanted smoke. Lo pushed through the crowd savagely until he reached his brother's side, who was squared off with about ten 'Bout Money Boys.'

"Fuck you, pussy niggas, swang!" Rod shouted as he held his hands up in front of him ready for combat.

Out of nowhere about seven of Rod's partners from his clique 'Been 'Bout A Check' pushed up and off rip, threw their hands up letting it be known they came to hook. Seeing that their chance to jam was over, the 'Bout Money Boys' fell back as administration and the resource officers pulled up on the scene and dispersed the crowd of onlookers.

Rod and Lo went down to a park that was located down the street from the school. They posted up and laughed about how shook them boys were when they pulled out and what they would do to them once they caught up with them. Lo and Rod headed to the Marta train station knowing Ms. Jones wasn't gonna let them get back on the bus after the stunt Lo had pulled. Both dread headed boys walked down the steps of the train station heading towards the platform and waited for the train to pull up. After waiting about fifteen minutes, killing time by talking to other students from the school, a train finally pulled up. Lo and Rod got on the train and chose to sit across from each other in the sparsely occupied cart of the train.

Lo looked at his brother who had his head back with his eyes closed and thought about all they'd been through.

Rod was a little darker compared to Lo's light-brown complexion. He also had eyes as black as coal while Lo had soft brown eyes, slanted in an angle, giving off the impression that he was mixed with Chinese. Lo was also a few inches taller than Rod, but Rod was a lot more violent and hardheaded when it came to authority – a part of his character he dubbed '*the fuck shit.*' Something he had taught Lo to accept as they grew older.

They were very different in appearance, but the two were like night and day. When you saw one, you would see the other. They did everything together from fighting, eating and even fucking the same girls, but what brought them even closer was how they struggled to win and stand tall against life together every day. They possessed a band that was unbreakable, something they had shared since they were in diapers. Being that they were the only two kids their mother had it came naturally for them to bond with each other. Their mother, Samantha was what you called a smoker – someone who did drugs but kept themselves presentable.

Samantha had a streak in her life before she had damn near overdosed from the use of crack when she had done everything from selling pussy to stealing from family members to get high. During those times, she got pregnant twice by two different men, she suspected were the fathers. But due to them disappearing she had no way to stake a claim and simply dealt with her kids the best way she could. This made Samantha cruel and neglectful, so the two grew up being abused physically and mentally. This pushed them toward creating ways to communicate less with their mother hoping this would keep her in good spirits.

Lo was fifteen and Rod was sixteen, but no one knew outside of school because of how they carried themselves. The facial hair they had given them that mature look as well. Lo kept his nicely trimmed while Rod thugged his out to match his rough character. Lo was more of a suave type and Rod was a true admirer of the Rastafarian culture and carried himself as if he were Jamaican.

'*College Park Station,*' announced the loudspeaker as it came to a stop.

Both brothers got off the train and weaved through people as they climbed the steps heading to the main level of the station where the buses were.

"Lo—Rod!" screamed a familiar voice that Rod wished he hadn't heard, knowing he would have to make good of his promise honestly not feeling up to it plus the pill had him on some war shit.

The two brothers turned their attention to a group of girls with Rod's latest smash Kissy Pooh leading the pack. Kissy Pooh was some real smash from the Pittsburgh neighborhood located in zone 3 of the city of Atlanta. Shawty had Asian features, mainly her eyes that gave her barely passing face something to look at. Kissy Pooh had a real body and her ass made her worthy of a nigga's time. But she had no brains, she was dumb ghetto and animated. She stood with her hands on her voluptuous wide hips with her gold micro braids pulled back into a ponytail.

"Shawty, what's good?" Rod asked as he walked up and disarmed Kissy Pooh with a kiss on the forehead as he wrapped his arms around her and squeezed her soft fat ass.

Lo stared at the other girls seeing that out of the two there was a girl, he had been seeing at school, who he had always wanted, but could never get. Chante Lovemore stood in her school attire, with pink puma shoe's talking to the short girl Lo knew as Shanna. Shanna was about 5'11, with long, sandy brown hair and green eyes, a petite small frame and a lil' nice ass on her. But she couldn't compare with Stacey who was 5'6, with bug firm titties that sat up and were accentuated by her flat stomach that led to her robust hips that had a donkey's ass attached to them. Stacey had her hair in a sexy, short cut that brought out her beautifully curved face, dimples, Colgate smile, and light hazel brown eyes. Lo knew the game Gods had looked out and let her fall into his path, so, he wasn't gonna fuck her today.

"What's up, Lo?" Shanna said looking at Lo with nothing but lust in her eyes.

"Ain't shit. How about you?" Lo replied with no enthusiasm in his voice sending a signal out that wasn't nothing poppin' between them as he openly stared at Stacey while she fiddled with her Metro phone, avoiding eye contact with Lo knowing he wanted her.

Stacey had been clocking Lo too, but as a lady and a beautiful one at that, she never made the first move. She found out the hard way neither did Lo, so she figured only destiny could bring them this close and it bothered her after so long. Now after all the pondering and wondering, they had finally crossed paths.

"Oh, you can't speak?" Lo asked bravely walking up on Stacey, putting one finger under her chin and lifting her head slowly until their eyes met causing a language to pass between them.

"Yeah, I can speak. What kind of question is that?" Stacey smiled.

"Oh, somebody got a new man!" Kissy Pooh squealed while wrapped in Rod's arms watching the interaction between the two as they communicated.

"Girl shut up, Lo' don't want her," Shanna said.

She wanted Lo just as bad as he wanted Stacey. Sensing the hate from Shanna, Stacey stepped on her tip toes and gave Lo a quick peck on his lips.

"Okaaay!" Rod said liking what he was seeing go down as the two ladies competed for his brother.

"Look, we 'bout to hit the spot before mom dukes get off work. Y'all wanna come?" Lo asked knowing it was either do or die. He just had to have Stacey who he had draped his arm around.

"Yeah, we gon' go," Kissy Pooh spoke making a choice that went unchallenged by the other girls.

"Let's go, the eighty-three just pulled up," Rod said, indicating the Marta Bus that took them to Stone Wall Tell Rd.

****

The sky was clear with no clouds, but oddly relaxing as the sun beat down on the Earth as the five individuals headed up the street toward Lo's and Rod's house. Though their momma was on Section 8, she still caught a nice home in the suburbs of metro-Atlanta. It was a long way from the run-down projects they had lived in for so many years. Where they could barely leave out of the house because of the violence in the streets, and they always had to sneak out when their mother was high. When they moved into the New Landing subdivision, it was still not a fully completed project, but as soon as the two malevolent boys could get out of there, they terrorized the neighborhood, burglarizing home after home kicking abandoned houses open, and gaining acceptance from other kids who were enticed and beguiled by their bad boy manner.

The Fulton County police had targeted the two after numerous speculation on the probability they were behind all the madness in the area that was non-existent before they invaded the neighborhood. But the boys were too slick, and they hated Fulton County Police. So, whenever they came sometimes, they called them for the hell of it and threw eggs or shot paintball guns at their cars fleeing on foot as officers exited their patrol cars to give chase. The group walked down the driveway to the nice four-bedroom brick house with the nice well- maintained lawn. Rod opened the front door knowing it was always opened day in and day out, something they both wished their mother would stop doing.

"Shhh!" Rod said, holding his finger to his mouth instructing the girls as they stepped onto the hardwood foyer.

A golden chandelier hung over them and a dining room set to their left that their mother never allowed them to sit in or walk through. The china dining room set was one of the things that had gotten salvaged from the fire set by Lo' that had burned their apartment building down five years ago and she cherished the set more than them it seemed at times. Rod smelled chicken in the air and knew his mom's latest boyfriend was cooking dinner.

"Rod, Lo', y'all badasses bet not be sneaking nobody in here!" Joe who was close to 350 pounds said from the kitchen.

"Fuck!" Lo' muttered under his breath, ushering the girls up the stairs.

"Ain't nobody sneaking nobody in the house," Rod lied as he sacrificed himself to go disable Joe's nasty ass ways.

'Lame ass, nigga,' Rod thought as he headed off.

On the second floor of the house Lo' led the girls to Rod's room that was located at the end of the carpeted hall and opened the door to see a qqaueen-sized bed with Family Dollar silk covers on them, a wood dresser set with a Dolby digital stereo sitting on the biggest one in front of the bed. Posters of Bob Marley, a picture of Huey P. Newton and Geronimo Pratt, the Apache war chief framed the walls of Rod's room.

As the girls sat down, Lo' walked to Rod's closet, opened it and bent down to retrieve a growing weed plant that looked to be about three months old. Lo' sat it on the dresser that had a mirror attached to it, then turned as the girls watched him curiously – never before seeing a weed plant. He bent under the bed to retrieve a spray bottle with water in it, then sprayed the plant down until he was satisfied, then opened the only window in the room and sat it on the ledge to get some sun.

"You look like you know what you doing?" Shanna said as she laid back on the bed on her side watching Lo'.

Shanna was from California and knew good weed from a mile but had never smoked. She was too scared of what would happen if her mother found out.

"What it look like?" Lo' retorted before taking his shirt off displaying his slightly muscled body that made the girls google at him.

Lo' threw the shirt in the corner of the room, then opened the bottom dresser, pulled it all the way out and retrieved the dime sack of weed and a Philly blunt they had stashed there.

Turning, Lo' threw the blunt and weed at Kissy Pooh knowing she knew how to roll because he had blown her head off at school a few mornings before they went to class. Rod entered the room elated knowing he was finally about to smash Kissy Pooh's thick, freaked out ass. He closed the door behind him, took off his shirt and threw it on the black wrap-a-round couch that set on the third floor of the house where they had chosen to take the girls Rod then walked over to the entertainment center opened a drawer, selected a CD and put it into his PlayStation 2. He turned it on and a few seconds after choosing options a woman named Pinky fucking another woman named Diamond Cuts in the ass with a dildo while she gave head to another woman played.

"Yo' freak ass!" Stacey said with a mischievous grin on her face never taking her eyes off the television as the sexual scene played out.

Kissy Pooh finished rolling the blunt, positioned herself so Rod could sit between her legs and pulled off her khaki pants revealing the blue booty shorts she had on.

Rod sat in between Kissy Pooh's thick, brown thighs after accepting the blunt in her outstretched hand. Lo' handed Rod the bottle of honey that they smothered their blunts with before smoking them which caused them to burn slow and a lighter. Lo' sat on the edge of the bed facing the TV as Stacey sat behind him sitting in Indian style getting turned on by the looks of pleasure on the porno stars faces.

"Hold up!" Lo announced as he got up from the bed and left the room, then came back with a wet rolled up towel that he pushed under the closed door to seal off the room making sure all smoke went out the window.

Rod flicked the lighter, lit the blunt and puffed on the purple haze inhaling deeply as Kissy Pooh played with his dreadlocks and neck. Rod blew smoke o's in the air from the potent weed as he mellowed from only three puffs of the weed. Kissy Pooh accepted the sticky blunt and pulled on it three times expertly, then passed it to Stacey who hesitated but accepted the blunt.

"You look scared," Lo' said as he peeled the blunt from her hands. "I'ma blow you a shotgun."

"*A shotgun?*" Stacey asked with a quizzical expression that only made her look more naïve and beautiful at the same time.

Lo' put the blunt in his mouth with the side she pulled from pointing in her direction and beckoning her forth. Stacey opened her mouth and Lo' grasped her head and blew smoke in her mouth. She inhaled and coughed before holding up her hands letting him know she was good.

"I want a shotgun, too!" Shanna said as she crawled across the bed toward Lo' on her hands and knees.

Lo' leaned forward without a word and blew Shanna a shotgun that caused her to wheel away, choking harshly. Taking the blunt out of his mouth and taking a toke, Lo' said, "You can't even handle a lil' shotgun. You better be careful what you ask for." Lo' then pulled on the blunt two more times before passing it back to Rod.

They smoked the blunt to the end and were greatly satisfied and horny from watching the flick as the scenes went from one and two to five on five, and two on one. Lo' decided this was his chance, he stood and pulled Stacey to her feet who didn't resist. They were oblivious to the jealousy that flashed in Shanna's green eyes as they exited the room.

Shanna muttered the word, "Bullshit." Then let her head hit the soft pillows of Rod's bed as Rod and Kissy Pooh lay on the side of the bed on the floor on the verge of fucking right there in the open.

Lo' opened his mother's room that was decked with green decoration from the four-poster bed to the big cotton stuffed chair to the footstool that sat in front of it. Lo' decided he wouldn't fuck Stacey on his mother's bed – the sin itself was big enough. He took her to the footstool and sat down as Stacey without words came out of her shirt, revealing her D-cup breasts that were trapped behind the red, lace bra she wore. As she undid the bra, Lo' unbuckled her khaki jeans and pulled them down her creamy chocolate legs. Lo' looked at Stacey's pussy print and leaned in to kiss her pierced belly button as he rubbed his hands over her bare backside.

Stacey stepped back, kicked off her pink Puma's, her khaki's, then rolled down her blue thong and tossed it in a pile onto the floor. She positioned herself doggy style as Lo' stood to come out of his khaki's. Lo' stared at the pink slit between Stacey's legs and desire overwhelmed him. He stepped toward Stacey with nothing on but some socks, grabbed Stacey's tooted up ass and pushed against her, teasing her pussy with the tip of his dick.

Stacey looked back with lust in her eyes and an expression that Lo' would always remember when he thought about her. Stacey reached between her legs, oblivious to the fact that Lo didn't have a condom on, too caught up in the moment to realize and guided him into her young sweet pussy. She put a deep arch in her back as Lo began to alternate between short and long strokes.

"I been wanting to fuck you since I first saw yo' sexy ass," Lo' said as he quickened his thrust, slamming into Stacey's ass watching her ass jiggle from the impact of their collision.

"Mmm," Stacey moaned, unable to produce any other sounds as she took good dick.

"Mmm, you gon' be mine now!" Lo' said as he gripped Stacey's small waist and held her while he stroked her, preventing her from falling off the footstool as he rammed in and out of her from the back like a jack-rabbit.

Smack! Smack!

Their skin sounded off throughout the room as Lo' who was still geeked up from the X-pill zoned out as he fucked Stacey from the back.

"Ouch, mmm—ahhh," Stacey moaned as she bounced forth, clutching the chair in front of her for support as Lo' fucked her like no other man had.

"This my pussy understand?" Lo' asked as he long stroked Stacey, going deeply as possible at the last second of every thrust.

"Mmhmm," Stacey moaned, nodding her head as she looked back at Lo' as he fulfilled her needs. Feeling the point of no return, Lo' slid in and out of Stacey's wetness and tightness.

Smack! Smack!

"Aaahhh," Lo' moaned as his seed shot into Stacey's pussy.

Lo' pulled out slowly as his penis became tender and backed away from Stacey watching her just stay in the position because she was scared, she would fall standing on her two legs.

"Lorenzo, what the fuck is going on in here!" his mother shrieked, standing in the doorway with her mouth agape at the two butt naked teens, one whom she didn't know.

"Bitch get the fuck out of my house!" Lo's mother shouted as she stood in the doorway with her work clothes on and menace in her eyes. Stacey quickly dressed and ran past Lo's mother with her head down. "Motherfucker, you get out too and don't take shit you didn't buy!"

As Lo' walked past his mother, she slapped him with so much force he almost cocked back and hit her back.

"Do it motherfucker!" his mother shouted.

Lo' dropped his hand, went to his room, grabbed a Nike bookbag and stuffed his stash and a few clothes in the bag. Then headed downstairs with rage in his eyes, before he could open the door, he heard, "You too, motherfucker! You got these hoes in my house like you pay some bills or something! Get the fuck out and take them two hoes with you!"

Seconds later, Shanna and Kissy Pooh, who was fixing their clothes, headed down the stairs with gloom on their faces from the treatment they were receiving.

Boom!

"Oh, motherfucker you wanna fight?"

Boom! Boom!

The house resounded as the sounds of a struggle went on upstairs between Rod and his mother.

"Go outside and wait for us," Lo' commanded as he ran up the stairs toward the commotion.

Just as Rod's hand was about to come down and hit their mother, Lo' screamed, "Bruh, don't do it! That's what she wants you to do!"

Rod stared at his brother with deep darkness in his blood-streaked face from where his mother had tried to gauge his eyes out. He dropped his fist as his mother scampered to her feet and ran downstairs toward the kitchen,

Rod took another measured breath and then quickly snatched up a few things he needed before heading down the stairs hot on Lo's trail. Just as Rod was about to go through the door something told him to turn around. When he did he witnessed his mother lodge her arm back and throw a knife toward him. Rod stepped quickly to the side as the knife flew past his face and landed on the ground in front of the door.

Before closing the door, Rod said with hate in his heart, "Have a nice life you, miserable bitch!" He slammed the door rattling the house.

Chapter 2

After all the commotion, Shanna threw a fit and called a cab to take her home without having any money, leaving them to think she had gone crazy because she had no money to pay the fare and could possibly go to juvy. That didn't stop them from heading to an abandoned house in the neighborhood a street over from where their mother lives. It was nightfall now as Lo' held Stacey and Rod held Kissy Pooh in their arms as they laid on the fresh carpet and stared out of the blindless windows, staring at the star-filled sky letting their thoughts drifted off far away into the galaxy.

Rod was the first to speak, "Life is so unpredictable. You have to stay ready for any blow that comes or you will fail, and no one will ever remember you or have compassion for you."

Silence filled the air for a while, then Lo' said as he rubbed Stacey's heart-shaped face with his right hand while she laid on her stomach with her head resting on his chest, "It's a cold world and not many will understand until the end presents itself in their lives."

Stacey held up her head and looked Lo' in his face illuminated by the light from the stars and said, "My step-mom put me out today."

Lo' looked down at her and the pieces fell into their respected places. He knew why she was so forthcoming when Kissy Pooh said they were coming with them. Shit was real in the streets and only the strong survived.

"Sometimes I be on some more shit. You can't even trust your own mama and she the one brought you in this world," Kissy Pooh sniffled as she sat in a sitting position and began wiping tears from her face, wondering if they had any idea she was selling herself on Metropolitan to feed herself and her child. Also, she had to take care of her brothers and sisters, this was the real reason she had gotten held back so many times in school. But no one would understand the chaos in her life at least that is what she felt. So, she never spoke on it instead she turned to drugs, partying and sex.

"Life is full of questions that we will never be able to answer," Rod spoke.

He was a very critical thinker when it came down to life, he always read and self-educated himself as much as possible because he knew that with knowledge was power, and power evolved into wealth. That was something he felt was worth his life and his precious time, so he indulged immensely in the study of great men, history of empires today and past, and any other thing that would allow him to get him and Lo' in the position they deserved in life.

"I know that's right, but what you gonna do about a place to stay? You can't just stay in here. We ain't got nothing to eat – no water or nothing." Lo' stated, not knowing that Kissy Pooh knew exactly what to do with Stacey's pretty ass and that was put on her on the track.

"I got her, don't worry about her. When we come back tomorrow, we gon' bring y'all something to eat," Kissy Pooh said as she played with Rod's dreads, who had now positioned himself between Kissy Pooh's legs with his head on her lap.

No one said anything else for a long period of time as they all contemplated their futures, their fears, and ways to quell the pain that dwelled within their souls from the coldness of everyday life in the streets.

****

"Their go, mama," Lo' said as she walked down the street the next morning.

Fog filled the air, but it was still visible and added a chill to the summer morning. Rod looked down the street and knew not one reason to be happy to see her. Lo' stopped on the side of the street, hoping their mother would have forgiven them by now and would let them come back home. Rod kept walking knowing their mother. She pressed the gas adding more speed to the van as she passed Lo', leaving him with a heart shattered into a thousand pieces. Any warmth she once had in her heart for them had gone cold and they were on their own to face this cruel world.

Rod stopped, turned around and saw that his brother had taken a seat on the edge of the sidewalk and put his head in his lap. His dreads were hanging down the sides of his legs as he wrapped his arms around his knees.

"*Strength, resilience and ambition*," Rod repeated in his head as he walked back toward his younger brother and sat down.

Rod pulled out a half-smoked blunt, the last of the ounce they had and lit it with the red Bic lighter before putting it back in his pocket. The day was May 31, 2018, and it was Rod's birthday. He had just turned seventeen. He exhaled the weed, oblivious to the fact that cars were passing by and they could possibly be reported for smoking in public being that they were underage. Rod didn't give a fuck about anything – not his mother, his future, or shit else, except Lo'. He wanted his younger brother to be successful no matter how their lives spawned out of control. Whether he became successful legally or illegally as long as he took back from these pussy ass crackers and the government, they set up to keep their kind castrated and lost to the streets.

"The struggle defines man, bruh, and once you embrace the struggle, you see there is only one way to go when the bottom has become your way," Rod said passionately as he passed the blunt to Lo' who raised his head the moment his brother began to speak, knowing if no one else in the world could bring peace to the chaos that constantly threatened their sanity, it was his big brother. Someone who was more like a father to him.

Before pulling the blunt, Lo' said, "The struggle is something we've been through since we were babies. Something that placed itself in our path so we'd be able to survive the now."

Rod nodded his head up and down knowing that Lo was a good listener, who at first used to cry all the time when their mother would leave them in roach-infested section 8 apartments earlier in their lives. Or when she would bring different men to the apartments only to end up getting beaten by one of the men. Out of all the things that frightened them both was when drug dealers who their mother owed would come kicking and beating on the door threatening to do violence, demanding a dead limit for their money. As their mother sat in the living room too geeked to even realize their life was in danger right along with hers.

Throughout those tough times, Rod made sure Lo' ate by going to stores and stealing what could be carted back in his little hands, he even stole clothes from time to time when back to school periods came around. Through all the fights with kids who laughed about their cheap clothes, awkwardness, and sometimes coming home badly bleeding from getting jumped by large groups of kids. As the incidents happened more frequently the two grew accustomed to the fact that they were hated, and it was beyond repair. No one embraced them, they played alone, they didn't own bicycles, dirt bikes, go-carts, and they didn't get to play recreational sports. They didn't have girlfriends growing up, so they became outcasts which forced their bond to grow stronger because with every trial and tribulation they saw they had each other and didn't need anybody else.

They started hustling with each other, they lost their virginity at the same time with the same girl in one of the numerous abandoned houses around the neighborhood. They smoked their first blunt together in which they were caught doing and had bruises on them to this day bringing them back to that day. They went to juvy their first time together, and almost everything else two brothers would do with each other.

A car stopped in front of them. It was a 2003 red Honda Civic, the windows rolled down and their partner Ronnie's mama Moe poked her head out the window and said, "Y'all badass done got put out again?" She looked them in their eyes knowing in her heart it wasn't right but a lotta shit wasn't right about life.

"Yeah," Rod stated simply as he blew a thick cloud of smoke out his mouth comfortable with Moe, who they sold and smoked weed with on the regular. One of the perks growing up fast in the streets was people respected you the way you presented yourself.

Moe was short for Moesha, she and her five kids were from Tampa, Florida. Word was, Moe was so addicted to coke she lost everything, packed all she had in an Astro van and fled to the city to start over with the help of the welfare department, something family members who had moved out of Florida a while ago had put her onto.

Moe was thirty-one, had red short dreads, and stood 5'2, 180 pounds and had mocha skin. They looked at Moe like a big sister and she treated them as she would her own by feeding them and giving them shelter when they had gotten kicked out of the house. Even though they could pull up at her house, the two still didn't feel it was right and didn't abuse the hospitality she offered. They decided instead to get it out of the streets and only as a last resort would they turn to her.

"You know y'all welcomed to my house, and let me hit that blunt," Moe stated.

She had dropped coke and picked up weed to deal with her reality – something she did at least three or four times a day. Moe was on section 8 too, so she had a little spending room and could balance her weed habit with her bills, responsibilities, and obligations. Knowing that Moe would pull up on them later, Rod hit the blunt one more time, stood up, walked toward Moe and gave her the blunt.

"We gon' just use your shower, wash and change our clothes, then we out of there," Rod said as he leaned on the car watching Moe as she smoked the rest of the blunt.

"That's okay, I got some extra breakfast on the table for y'all. I saw y'all earlier and decided to fix y'all a plate. It's in there, gon' 'head, I'm 'bout to head to the social security department. I should be back in an hour. Make sure Camry is fed," referring to her one-year-old little girl who she knew Rod adored.

"A'ight," Rod said as him and Lo' began heading toward her house to handle their business.

****

"Fuck all that! We might as well break in some shit before we go meet them hoes," Lo' argued as they walked around the corner onto Main Street.

The sun was beaming down hard this afternoon, it was the perfect opportunity to break into some shit Lo thought. Rod figured he was always on some hot shit, but then he thought about the situation and decided to go along with the plot knowing exactly what house they would hit.

"A'ight, but we gotta play by my rules," Rod said looking at his younger brother waiting for confirmation.

"Bruh, you already know I'm down for whatever," Lo' replied ready to do some shit to put some money in their pockets.

Lo' thought about the connections they had stumbled across trimming in Five Points downtown. Some African named Mutumbo paid top dollar for all electronics no matter the year, make, or model if they worked. The two couldn't figure out why the Africans would want the shit but didn't give a fuck long as they got what they wanted out of the deal. They usually targeted TVs, cell phones, laptops, game systems, clothes, and money. Rod ran down the plan as they walked out of the subdivision, turned right and headed down Stone Wall Tell road until they got to a hidden path through some woods and looked both ways before they headed into the well-worn path. As they came out of the wooded area they were in the backyard of a row of houses in the Forest Downs subdivision.

"That house, right there," Rod pointed to the back of a nice ranch-style house with no patio, just a door that led inside the kitchen and a window that was over the kitchen sink.

The two looked around to see if anyone was watching, after seeing that the coast was clear they walked up to the house and peered into the house making sure no one was home. Seeing that no one was in the house, they went back and forth about a way to break into the house coming to an agreement after nearly two minutes of debating. Rod took off his white Footlocker T-shirt, wrapped it around his hands, walked up to the kitchen window and swiftly punched the glass with his arm going through cutting himself. His Adrenaline was pumping as Rod stuck his arm back into the window, unlatched the window and raised it up. Lo' helped Rod through the window. Rod scooted through the window, jumped off the sink onto the floor, went to the backyard door and opened it for Lo' to come in. Lo' walked through the door and whistled at the décor of the stylishly furnished home.

"All this shit with no alarm," Lo' said looking at the flat- screen that mounted the wall, the laptop scrawled on a table in the center of the living room along with much more valuable shit that they could take.

"Damn," Rod muttered, looking at the small trickle of blood running down his arm.

"You a'ight, big bro?" Lo' asked who had just noticed the blood running down his brother's arm.

"I'm straight," Rod said as he headed to the sink, rinsed his arm and let Lo' tie it.

After this, the two began to plunder the house with the skill of two professional cat burglars, bagging everything worth anything, putting it into the hockey bags they found in the garage. Lo' was in the master bedroom picking up jewelry, stuffing it into his short's pockets. Stopping, Lo' picked up a picture with a beautiful lady on it and man dressed in a tuxedo, holding the woman's full attention. She looked like she was Cuban.

'Damn, shawty got a fat ass!' Lo' thought as he put the picture down and returned to the drawers, stopping when he discovered what he figured was the woman's underwear and began rambling through her panties, thongs, G-strings and boy shorts. Imagining what she would look like in them, his hands went deeper and hit something hard. He pulled it out and came face to face with a dildo. Lo' shrieked, threw the dildo in the air and it landed on the bed.

"What's up?" Rod asked quickly appearing at the door of the bedroom with an alarmed expression on his face. Lo' pointed at the dildo with a screwed face. Rod burst into laughter and said, "Shawty must ain't getting that dick right."

Lo turned, leaving Rod there laughing as he rambled through the other dressers in the room, finding $2,000 in fresh twenties and a .38 snub-nosed pistol with a pistol-grip, the first pistol he had ever scored for.

"Jackpot!" Lo' said as he finished going through the room taking a couple more valuables and stuffing them in the black hockey bag.

"Let's go!" Rod screamed after seeing a car pull into the driveway of the house.

Lo' rushed down the stairs and jumped down the rest of the steps just as Rod ran past him, black hockey bag in tow. Lo' ran behind his brother out the back door, leaving it wide open as they ran ensuring their getaway.

＊＊＊＊

"Boy, where y'all get all this shit from?" Kissy Pooh asked as she sat the two bags of Chinese food on the ground of the abandoned house, indicating to all the electronics Rod and Lo' had scattered across the floor of the empty bedroom with a window that gave a view of the driveway and anyone who approached the cul-de-sac.

"You dumb nosey, come here!" Rod demanded as he sent a text message to their African clientele Mutumbo letting him know all the merchandise they had and the price he wanted for it all. Kissy Pooh walked over to Rod in a Juicy Couture shirt, booty shorts and a pair of Greek sandals that showcased her pretty feet.

"Turn around," Rod commanded.

Being the freak she was Kissy Pooh turned around slowly and seductively, giving Rod a nice view of her fat ass that had *Juicy* written across the green shorts she wore. Rod slapped Kissy Pooh's ass causing her to shriek, then turn around and hit Rod playfully on the arm. Stacey had on a new outfit as well, a pair of *Ed Hardy* jeans with a matching shirt that showed every curve of her full breasts and a pair of pink Number 8 Jordan's. Stacey walked over to Lo' where he was smoking a blunt. She sat the food she brought for him down, then sat down next to him, took out the food and began feeding Lo' wordlessly.

"Bitch you think you doing something," Kissy Pooh said jokingly and giggled with her friend about how she was treating her man.

"Mind your business," Rod said before he slapped Kissy Pooh on the ass again, but this time a little softer and watched her ass jiggle.

Rod looked at his phone just as it vibrated, then opened the message he'd just received from Mutumbo who told him he could do that and asked where he wanted them to meet. Rod texted him back and gave him the explicitly explained directions. Rod grabbed Kissy Pooh by the hand

and led her to the room next door as she smiled the whole way, knowing she was about to get some dick.

"Freaky ass," Stacey said smiling at her friend who had brought her in like a sister and showed her how to make money from what all men loved which was pussy.

Stacey didn't feel comfortable at first, but once she experienced her first trick and got one hundred dollars. She quickly caught on fast and her worries and fears dissipated. Some of the tricks didn't even want no pussy. They just paid her to eat her out and talk to them. Stacey was surprised at the things a man would do to get the attention of an attractive female. Her parents didn't bring her up to see the world as she saw it now, but when her own father chose a bitch that wasn't her biological mother over her. She decided to piss on everything he ever taught her and get money the only way she could which was using her looks and flashing a little ass.

Stacey liked Lo, she didn't want him to know she was prostituting, feeling like it would destroy all the respect he had for her. Little did she know, Lo' already knew from her clothes, new hair, phone and the sparkle in her eyes that she had been introduced to the streets in a way Kissy Pooh could only reveal to her, but he wouldn't judge her by that. He would judge her by how she performed in his presence.

"Ah, Mmm," Kissy Pooh moaned loudly as she beat on the walls. "Rod, Rod—ohhh, Rod!" Kissy Pooh filled the air with harmonious sexual sounds letting them know Rod was laying the dick down.

"Flexin' ass," Lo' said as he took another mouth full of the food, enjoying the feeling Stacey gave him.

It was new, he had never been fed by a woman before. It was just something about Stacey that stirred his loins and made him want to fuck the shit out of her every time he looked in her hazel brown eyes.

"Shawty, you beautiful as a motherfucker," Lo' complimented out of nowhere which caused Stacey to show that beautiful dimpled smile that always made his heart flutter.

"You want some?" Stacey asked in a sexy voice, putting the empty container to the side, giving Lo' the Tropicana punch to wash down the food she had fed him.

Lo' picked the blunt up, lit it again and started smoking. He watched as Stacey pulled his semi-erect penis out of his Jordan shorts and started sucking him. Lo' puffed the blunt looking down as Stacey tried to suck his dick, something she clearly didn't know how to do.

Lo' said, "Slow down and open your mouth wide as you can so your teeth don't scrape my dick." Lo held Stacey's head and guided her up and down. "Use some spit to lubricate my dick. It makes it easier for you to deep throat," Lo' instructed as he watched Stacey get the hang of it and began serving him as if she was born to suck dick.

Fully aroused, Lo' pushed Stacey's head up, then stood up and pulled his pants down, his dick pointed straight, mesmerizing Stacey as she stared at it like it was a piece of gold. Lo' walked up on Stacey while she was still on her knees, grabbed her micro-braids and pulled her head toward his penis until her mouth was wrapped around his dick, then started pumping in and out of her mouth. Stacey let saliva slide out of her mouth, lubricating Lo's thick meat as she massaged his balls to slap against her chin. Stacey pushed Lo' away, then stood and stripped out of her clothes, not caring that the door was open. She got butt naked, laid on the floor on her back and spread her legs wide open, then began rubbing her clit while staring Lo' in the face as he jacked his dick still shining from the saliva she left on it.

Lo' dropped to his knees, picked up Stacey's legs and held them in the air as he positioned his dick to enter her. Stacey grabbed his dick through her legs and guided him into her moist pussy. Lo' entered Stacey with ease, sliding all the way in until he could no more and held himself there enjoying the feeling of her warm pussy as it wrapped around his dick. Stacey arched her back as Lo' began beating her pussy relentlessly sliding all the way in, ramming his dick in and out of her.

"Ohhh, oooh!" Stacey moaned, she grabbed the carpet with her hands as she made love faces with her eyes closed, unable to open them.

Lo' pushed both of her legs all the way back until they touched the ground and slightly stood on his feet, leaning over her, and slammed his dick in and out of her repeatedly trying to dig a hole in her pussy.

"Ahhh, fuck meee!" Stacey screamed, she lost control of herself, feeling a mixture of pain and pleasure as Lo' touched a spot in her pussy that no man ever had.

"Ahhh!" Lo' moaned as he came deep inside Stacey, unable to hold back any longer.

"You just fucked the shit out of my friend," Kissy Pooh giggled as she stood in the door without Rod who had gone out the door to meet, Mutumbo.

"Bitch you nasty! You watching us fuck?" Stacey screamed feeling as if she was in heaven and falling in love with Lo' the more she stayed around him.

Lo' pulled his semi-erect dick put of Stacey and fell on the side of her on his back, oblivious to both, thinking about how good Stacey's pussy was.

"Bitch, put some clothes on!" Rod said after popping back up from hollering at Mutumbo. Walking into the room, seeing his brother and Stacey naked, Rod said, "What the fuck? Y'all about to have an orgy without me?"

Nah, nigga, you can't get none of this pussy. Shawty mine!" Lo' stated as he stood up and put his boxers back on with a serious expression on his face.

Rod held up his hands, then said, "Bruh, I'm just playing, but that play out there. Help me get this shit together."

Rod slyly looked at Stacey's naked body as she got dressed. Their eyes locked briefly, then Stacey looked away, feeling as if Rod has just stripped her back down to nothing with his eyes.

"Let's go then, nigga!" Lo' said as he finished putting the electronics in the hockey bag.

"A'ight," Rod replied as he thought about how easy it would be to smash Stacey for the check.

He knew what she was about. Kissy Pooh had shown him the videos she recorded of Stacey as she participated in a ménage-a-trois with two men, as she got her pussy ate by a female and many other explicit video clips that showed Stacey to be a real freak. Rod just wanted to fuck the lil' freak hoe and let her continue to play Little Red Robin Hood with his brother.

'*Nasty bitch.*' Rod thought as they headed out the door to go cash in with Mutumbo.

****

"Five thousand, bruh. That's all we got to our name, plus this lil' mufucka," Lo' said holding up the shiny .38 Revolver.

"Shit, we better off than we started," Rod' replied as they crept back around the abandoned house and went in through the window separately, making sure no one saw them.

Back in the house, they headed upstairs back to the master bedroom and found Kissy Pooh and Stacey looking at videos on Stacey's phone. Stacey immediately grabbed the phone and turned off the videos.

Lo looked at her suspiciously then asked, "What y'all looking at?"

"Nothing," Stacey replied quickly, fiddling with the phone.

"Shawty stop lying, let me see that phone," Lo' commanded as the air grew tense in the room.

Kissy Pooh and Rod knew what was on the phone and looked on.

"Fuck no!" Stacey refused, got up and tried to run out the door but was blocked by Lo'.

Stacey immediately threw the phone to Kissy Pooh who started deleting the videos as Lo' and Stacey wrestled. Rod stood there shaking his head, knowing how fucked up the world was especially for runaways. Lo' finally broke free of Stacey, ran up to Kissy Pooh and snatched the phone out of her hand. As he went through the phone, he saw that the videos had been deleted. He turned around angrily and marched, Stacey and slapped her in the face with a force so hard she hit the ground and held her face. Lo' then grabbed her by her hair, drug her out of the room to another room and slammed the door.

Rod just shook his head and asked Kissy Pooh as she sat on the floor trying to hear if Lo' was beating her friend. "I know you know where to get some weed from?"

Turning her head toward Rod she asked, "How much you trying to get baby?"

"I'm really trying to get about three bags of some gangsta med."

"Oh, that's it?" Kissy Pooh replied like she had seen more than that.

Rod didn't even respond, he just threw his phone at her roughly, letting her know to set up the play. Rod walked over to the only window in the room that gave light to the darkened house and stared out the window calculating a plan, knowing he needed a car to get money and knew D-Zee had a 1972 Cutlass Supreme for $1800. He made a mental note to holla at him the next day. Suddenly, the sounds of sex filled the house as Lo' and Stacey made up. Rod shook his head at his tender dick ass little brother but thought about how he had handled the situation about the videos and a smile stretched across his face. He prided himself for teaching the lil' nigga how to handle a bitch who got out of line.

Chapter 3

Rod whipped the metallic black Cutlass into the neighborhood called Pittsburg Community, drove down the darkened street, then made another left and stopped in front of what could only be a trap house.

"This the spot?" Rod asked Kissy Pooh who was sitting on the passenger side of the car.

"Yeah, nigga. How many times you gon' ask me that?" Kissy Pooh responded as she sent a text to let Kay know she had pulled up for the play.

It was dark outside, and the stars were out. They were the only things that gave a shed of light to the street they had turned on, being that the streetlights had long ago been shot out.

"Bruh, this shit don't even feel right," Lo' stated from the back seat with Stacey sitting beside him, honestly feeling the same way, but dared not speak not wanting to scare them with her insecurities.

"Ain't nothing gon' happen to y'all. These niggas fuck with me!" Kissy Pooh spoke confidently, just as a strange, tall dude walked up to the car.

Rod immediately opened the door, filling the darkened street with light and said to Kay, "What's good, my nigga?"

"Shit, you know, tryna make it to the next day," Kay answered throwing Kissy Pooh a lustful glance.

"Nigga, what the fuck you looking at? Handle ya business," Kissy Pooh stated.

She didn't even like Kay because he just gave off a sick vibe, plus he always wore the same clothes for two to three days at a time, but he always had some weed and that was enough to put the play together.

"Fuck you, where the money?" Kay asked turning his gaze back toward Rod, standing with his hands on the hood of the Cutlass staring at Kay who stood on the other side of the door.

"Bruh, this shit 'bout 'business. Whatever you and shawty got going, hold that shit down. But here the check, where the weed?" Rod asked as he began to fan through the assortment of money he had in his hand.

Eyes on the money, eye-balling the worth, Kay was satisfied and said, "Hold up, I 'll be right back with the weed." He left back down the driveway of the house he had come out of.

"Bitch, you gon' make me beat yo' ass," Rod said poking his head back in the car, glaring at Kissy Pooh.

Kissy Pooh rolled her eyes and turned her head to look out the window towards the direction Kay had gone, mad from the way Kay had just handled what was supposed to be strictly business.

"Bruh, fuck all that. You can deal with shawty later. Stay focused, we don't even know these niggas," Lo' said placing the .38 revolver on his lap, anticipating the fuck shit.

"You right. What's taking this bitch ass nigga so long?" Rod said, speaking to nobody in particular.

"He gon' be out, just chill," Kissy Pooh stated still looking off in the direction Kay had gone.

Clash! The glass on the driver's side of the Cutlass shattered out of nowhere as three men in black attire surrounded the car with guns drawn. The one who shattered the window reached for the driver's door and opened it, flinging it open, screaming, "Fuck nigga you already know what it is. Come on with it!"

Rod slammed his hands on the wheel as blood ran down his face from the shards of glass that cut him. Nobody moved in the car as Rod handed the bankroll over to the robber's hands. Rod tried to see if he could see the face of the robbers, but they all had ski-masks on making it impossible.

The gunman snatched the bankroll out of Rod's stretched hand and said, "You lucky I'on kill yo lil' bitch ass. Stay the fuck outta the burg sucka!" He backed away with the other's guns still drawn blending in with the darkness and making an escape.

Rod cranked the car up and peeled out of the neighborhood with rage shaking his body. Back on Metropolitan Parkway, Rod stopped the car right in front of the Run-and-Shoot basketball center and said coldly, "Y'all hoes get the fuck out my shit."

"But—" Kissy Pooh spoke.

She was cut off as Rod backhanded her with so much force it felt as if her front tooth had loosened. Blood seeped out her mouth as she opened the door with tears in her eyes.

Rod felt no remorse, then turned back and said, "You too, bitch! Get yo' freak ass up out my shit before I shoot you in the fuckin' face!"

Stacey looked at Lo' who wore an impassive look on his face knowing he wouldn't go against his brother for anyone. Stacey pushed the seat forward knowing she didn't have anything to do with what went on, but the coldness of Rod's eyes let her know she was an enemy. Stacey got out of the car and slammed the door. Rod hit the gas, speeding off into the night knowing they had just taken a major loss and those bitches were going to pay the piper one day.

"Bruh, them bitches set us up!" Lo' screamed as he banged his fist into the headrest of the passenger seat.

"I know, bruh. Them bitches gon' pay, but we gotta stay focused and count our losses with our blessings."

"That's some fuck shit."

"Life is some fuck shit," Rod shot back before pushing play on the CD player, filling the car with sounds of '*Webbie's Savage Life 2*' as they both contemplated their next move knowing it was back to the abandoned house until an avenue opened for them.

Chapter 4

It had been two weeks since they got robbed and things weren't looking any better for them. The lil' bit of money they did have was spent on food, gas and to repair the window on Rod's Cutlass. Their mother still was on the bullshit and didn't want to let them in. She had thrown the rest of their belongings into the streets in black garbage bags, letting them know without words it was most definitely a wrap. Lo' contemplated on going to their grandma's place which was their last hope. Rod was as stubborn as ever and said their grandmother was just as bad as their mother. Lo' agreed so they stayed in the bando, alternating from there to Moe's house where Rod kept his Cutlass when he wasn't driving it.

It was a Saturday night, they were back in the bando contemplating how they were going to strike. It had been hard to break in some houses since the people of the community had formed some type of neighborhood watch group and had been getting young nigga after young nigga locked up. So, they figured they would fall back until the heat died down.

"Bruh, I'm dumb hungry!" Lo' stated as he laid back on the carpet rubbing his hand across his rumbling stomach.

"Me too, lil' nigga, but we broke and I refuse to pull up at Moe's spot even though it ain't nothing to her," Rod replied as he stared at his phone as if something was gonna pop out of it and solve their problems.

"Let's rob the pizza man again," Lo' suggested sitting up looking for confirmation on the only plan he had.

"Shit, we ain't did that in a while. Might as well, huh?" Rod asked as he began scanning down his call-log in search for one of the numerous pizza numbers he'd added to his phone just for this purpose.

Looking up, Rod asked, "Pizza Hut or Papa John's?"

Lo' contemplated for a second, then said, "Domino's, bruh."

"A'ight, you always gotta be different," Rod said as he dialed the only Domino's number, he had listed in his phone and put it to his ear as it rang.

"Hi, yes this is Mr. Carmichael. My address is one-thirty-five Stone Lake drive. I would like two large hamburger pizzas, one medium pepperoni, fifty wings, and three boxes of cheese sticks. Well, yes, this is a big order. We're having a get-together, I will be paying cash. Oh, have a nice night and thank you also," Rod said imitating his best white man's voice, smiling as the worker of Domino's ate the game up. He ended the call, looked up and said, "Let's go, and you grab the food. I'ma handle everything else, okay?"

"Say no more, I got you. As hungry as I am, I'on want to do no talking anyway," Lo' replied as he headed to the dark bedroom behind his brother to go meet the pizza man with thoughts of eating a whole pizza by himself running through his head.

****

The 2005 Dodge Ram F-150 truck pulled up to a stop outside the abandoned house next door to the one Rod and Lo' were staying in. The driver peered up the driveway, saw no lights, and double checked the address of the order before pulling into the driveway thinking they might have the lights off waiting.

Tom had been working for Domino's for quite some time and had seen some of the craziest shit. Nothing amazed him anymore. He hoped it was one of those women who couldn't pay, but would swap a sexual favor, something he had grown to anticipate as a man in his forties, divorced twice and seldom ever got any pussy unless he paid. It suited him well because he had enough of that lovey-dovey shit anyway.

Tom opened the door of the truck and popped the glove compartment open, grabbing the .32 Revolver that the company issued due to numerous robberies that had occurred during deliveries. Tom didn't have those kinds of problems but he was a subordinate worker and followed protocol no matter how strange or severe it was, especially things concerning his safety. He tucked the steel under his blue work shirt and grabbed his hat, placing it on his bald head making sure he was presentable in case it was a lucky night. Satisfied, Tom grabbed the order and got out of the truck, closed the door and turned to walk the path leading to the front door. As he reached the door, Tom pushed the doorbell and heard the sound throughout the home. The door opened revealing two dread headed boys as Tom became disappointed knowing it wasn't a special night.

"How you guys doing, tonight? They told me y'all were having some big get together," the white man said trying to get a look over of Rod but was blocked by Lo's tall frame.

"Yeah, the rest of the company hasn't arrived yet. May we check our orders and make sure they're correct?" Rod asked, looking at the delivery man and any signs of suspicion.

"Sure," Tom stated as he handed the boxes containing their food to Lo' who immediately accepted them, then turned heading to the back of the house and out the door.

Rod faked like he had some money in the pocket of his Jordan shorts and came up quick with a lightning-fast punch that caught Tom in his chin. Tom reached out blindly as he was falling and pulled Rod down with him by mistake. The two began tussling on the pavement. Rod quickly took advantage of the situation by breaking the grasp the big man had him in and positioning himself on top of the man as he rained blow after blow to the man's face.

Tom started screaming, "Take the money – just take it!"

"Where it at fuck, nigga!" Rod shouted, continuing his assault on Tom's bloody face.

As Rod lifted to get off Tom so he could give the money, Tom pushed Rod backward sending him sprawling into the frame of the door. Tom scrambled up, reached under his shirt and recovered the .32 Revolver and without hesitation started firing the gun.

Boom! Boom! Boom! Boom!

Rod's body was racked with shot after shot, shaking his body violently as he slid to the ground. Tom, seeing he had killed the young man, began wheeling back toward the truck. Tom opened the door, got into the truck and grabbed the phone, dialing 911 letting them know what happened as he backed out of the driveway and fled the scene.

Hearing the gunshots, Lo' ran back down the small hill that led to the house they had just broken into, with all his might. His heart was pumping loudly in his chest as fear of the unknown engulfed his being. Rounding the house, Lo' jumped over the flower bed and ran through it until he was in the pathway that led to the front door. Lo' immediately stopped in his tracks and dropped to his feet at the sight of his brother and his condition.

"No," he whispered as he stared at his brother's blood-soaked body. The light from the sky made the scene even more horrific. Lo' got up and moved toward his brother, tears spilling down his face. Lo' dropped to his knees and gathered his brother who was barely breathing into his arms. "Bruh, you gon' make it. Don't die on me like this," Lo' said softly as he held his brother in his arms, blood soaking him from the numerous holes that were pumping blood.

"Bruh—keep—the—fuck—shit—alive—" Rod sputtered as he coughed up blood.

"Shhh, save your energy," Lo' said as he looked into his brother's eyes knowing he was dying and there wouldn't be any Miami trips in the summer, no shopping sprees in New York, no strip clubs, no nieces or nephews, and most devastating, that it was all real. Lo' leaned down, kissed his big brother's forehead and said, "Bruh, please don't die." As he whispered those words, Rod had taken his last breath. "Noooo—somebody help please, somebody help!" Lo' screamed as he began shaking his brother as if he could revive him.

Lo' heard the sirens but still refused to move even as they shouted for him to lay on the ground. He refused even as they threaten to shoot him, he refused, and it gave them no choice but to use force, and even then, Lo' refused until they zapped him with a Taser and everything went blank as he drifted off to the dark place he wished he could go forever.

Chapter 5

After sitting in the Fulton County police station with his mother, who he was surprised even showed up, the Sergeant finally grew tired of Lo's refusal to speak on the incident or the burglary they had committed.

"Fuck you, bitch! I ain't got shit to say!" Lo' screamed, his words could be heard throughout the entire department.

After several attempts to break the shield Lo' had put up, the Sergeant was green-lighted by the Lieutenant to go ahead and take Lo' to Metro Youth Department of Correctional facing charges on the incident with the pizza man. Since they couldn't without a shadow of a doubt point the finger at Lo', they didn't charge him with the burglary. Lo' sat in the back of the police cruiser lost in his thoughts as his heart continued to harden. He vowed to make sure the bitch who set them up got paid back because if that hadn't happened, Rod would still have been with them. He also vowed that he would continue striving, remember his brother's word and keep the fuck shit alive!

The cruiser finally slowed down as the gates of the juvenile facility loomed ahead. The cruiser turned left, pulled up to the gate and was told to halt as the officer checked under the car with a long-handled mirror. After that, he asked the officer what he was there for, then reported it to the main control and received instructions to let the cruiser through. The cruiser came to a stop in the middle of the admission part of the building and the police officer got out of the cruiser looking like a cop from *Reno 911* with his thick drooping beard and mirror tinted glasses.

"Let's go, boy," the white officer ordered after opening the door to the backseat of the cruiser.

Without a word, Lo' got out of the car and was escorted to the door. The police officer rapped on the door a few times, then an electronic click could be heard letting him know he could pull the door open. Lo' stepped inside the intake part of the juvenile facility with the officer. The intake officer, whom everyone knew as Zone 3 was standing behind the bulletproof glass of the control room looking down at Lo' with sympathy in her eyes. The heath of his brother had been on Channel 2 Action News. Ms. Zone 3 knew every kid that was a frequent visitor to the Youth Department of Correctional whether they were from the inner city or Metro-Atlanta. Ms. Zone 3 was a tall, dark-skinned, older lady who wore her hair short with a big nose and a big gap in her mouth, but her personality made her popular amongst the kids who could identify with her.

"Baby straighten up your face, everything gon' be alright. Are you alright? You don't need to be taken to Grady hospital or nothing, do you?" Ms. Zone 3 asked as she began sliding forms for the officer to fill out through a metal box that allowed people on the other side of the control center to get things and turn in weapons. Their business was far beyond dropping a juvenile off.

"I'm good," Lo' answered looking at the floor with his dreads hanging in a wild tangle mess as his mood continued to flare.

"Well, put him in that cell right there until we process his paperwork," the older lady instructed.

The officer took the handcuffs off Lo' and led him to the cell the lady was referring to. After popping the door open, Lo' walked in. The officer said, "Keep your head up, kid."

Lo' responded by flipping a bird at the officer and muttering, "Fuck you, cracker!" Which got a laugh out of the other boy who was sitting in the holding cell.

The officer slammed the door with anger in his eyes at Lo's comment. Lo' turned and walked to the bench that was made from cement and took a seat, dreads concealing his face. After some time, Lo' used a hand to swipe his long dreads out of his face and took a glance to his left where the other kid who laughed at his jest was sitting. His eyes found a brown-skinned kid who clearly was almost seventeen from the beard on his face and his face told of life in the streets. Catching the gaze toward him, the heavily muscled kid looked back with the same concentrated stare and felt the energy the kid gave off and it felt like his own.

Feeling the same energy Lo decided to break the silence. "What's up fool my name's, Rude," he said outstretching his hand.

The boy looked at his hand for a moment, went against his instinct and took hold of it before replying, "My name's, Pistol."

The two talked to each other through the entire orientation process, each knowing right then that a bond for whatever it was worth had been formed. Pistol leaned back on the wall as the reason why he was in there hit him in the face and ran his hands down his waved head over his face. Pistol shook his head and let out a tired sigh, then said, "Pussy ass police tryna say I killed the nigga who shot my brother last week. They ain't got no evidence so they had a young nigga as a witness who say he saw me point me out and to make matters worse they jumped out on me and caught me with a bomb of crack. Pussy ass police acting like they found a brick on me, this crazy, bruh! I just got out Eastman YDC about three months ago and here I am back in this motherfucka."

Silence filled the air for a moment, then Rude broke it by asking, "Where you from?"

"Shit, I'm from Dec," Pistol answered, referring to Decatur, Georgia, "But I be playing all around the city. They just knocked me on Simpson Road."

"Damn, bruh, I know you ain't tryna go through this bullshit again."

"Hell nah, nowhere in my plan was a trip to this bullshit anywhere in it," Pistol said giggling at his own joke, but Rude could find no humor in it.

The two continued to chop it up even as they were admitted to the intake area where they were sprayed with delicer, showered and given a blue jumpsuit.

"I hope we get the same dorm. I fuck with you, bruh. I knew that when I saw you, chump, that pussy ass cracker off. You was cut from the same cloth as me, and to be honest, if I hadn't seen that I would have never even spoken to you," Pistol revealed as they snacked on the sandwiches that the intake officer had brought them.

Rude nodded his head acknowledging and respecting Pistol for his truthfulness.

"Bruh, I do no fake kicking it either and I'm on some more shit, bruh, some fuck shit. So, it's either get down or lay down with me. I no longer possess the patience for bullshit. I want in or I'ma do me and wipe a nigga bitch or whoever nose clean if that's what it takes to get mine," Rude said as he looked over into Pistol's eyes trying to gauge his reaction to his words.

"The fuck shit, huh?" Pistol smiled knowing in his head he had just met one of the last dying breeds and he would put his all into helping establish and build whatever there was to be built by fucking with his newly acquired associate, Rude.

"Yeah, the fuck shit," Rude repeated as he leaned back in the chair with his finger on his temple, gazing at Pistol.

"The fuck shit then, nigga!" Pistol agreed, extending his hand one final time.

Rude took it without hesitation this time as he stared Pistol in the eyes to see if he saw any deceit, fakeness, game or any of the shit he didn't need in his circle.

Just as they dropped hands, the intake officer walked back into the room carrying their kits filled with towels, toothpaste, tissue, blankets, and other things they were supposed to have, then said, "Let's go, both of you are going to G-One. Don't be giving my officers no shit. I know both of you. I'll be down there to kick y'all ass if I hear anything."

"Who the fuck you talking to?" Rude said as he stood to his feet, much taller than the intake officer they knew as JCO Payne who was always talking shit and making time hard for kids who came to the juvenile.

"I'm talking to you now—" Before he could finish his words, Rude swung, hitting him square in the face causing the things he had in his hands to fly everywhere as he hit the ground. Pistol jumped in the fight and began stomping the guard.

"Fuck—nigga—you—better—watch—yo—mouth—" Rude warned after each stomp to Payne's head.

Somehow Payne managed to hit the code button on his radio and in less than two minutes JCOs swarmed the intake area. Without warning, they began putting hands on Rude and Pistol, who stopped resisting once they saw it was no win in their situation.

As they both laid on their stomachs with officers on top of them, they looked over at one another and Rude said, "Fuck shit!"

Pistol replied with a smile on his face, "Fuck shit!"

They were roughly picked up and escorted to G-1 where they were locked down in individual cells. Rude had a roommate, but Pistol didn't due to his history of violence.

****

Three weeks had passed since the incident in the intake and the only communication between Rude and Pistol was under the door of their rooms where they remained on lock-down. They were across the range from each other, so that made it easier to talk to one another under the door. Rude had a bunkmate who slept in a boat in the room with him. His name was Penny, he was Mulatto and Creole. Penny was from New Orleans. His family had moved to the states after the disastrous hurricane destroyed it. His family never returned as the allure of Atlanta became more enticing as the days had gone by which turned into years. Penny had lost two sisters, mother and the rest of his family except his father and brother to the flood. His brother, Round, had caught several bodies when they first moved to the city and was sentenced to life in prison, something that hurt Penny every day he opened his eyes.

His brother had taught him all he needed to know when it came to playing with fire, from shooting, aiming, cleaning guns, the use of different guns, and how to get money using them. Penny had gone on his first move at the age of eleven and shot his first man at the age of twelve. Penny was an evil-minded young nigga, Rude summed it up by all the fuck shit he had experienced that turned him cold and that suited Rude well because he was on the same shit.

Penny earned his name from his copper skin tone. He was 5'5, weighed 120 pounds soaking wet and was underestimated because of his size. But soon they found out after they woke up in E.R. that the young nigga was not to be fucked with. He played to win and often it wasn't fair. Penny stayed in the 4th Ward off Boulevard in a little two-bedroom apartment with his aging father who always had a bottle of some sort in his hands to ease the pain he constantly felt in his life. Something he told his son from time to time to quell his wanes, but they never fully extinguished them and the many trips to the doctor from his kidneys failing still didn't stop him from indulging in his pleasure. So, Penny gave up and watched his father take a closer step to his grave every day he woke up. Penny refused to sit back and watch his daddy die, so he turned to the streets for comfort and began robbing, stealing, and everything else to get money.

Rude grew to like the young nigga and Penny grew to like Rude in the short time they knew each other. They stayed up long hours of the night talking and playing cards, swapping stories about their lives and where they wanted to go and be in the future. They shared similar ambitions, but the one that meant the most was making it where they didn't have to wake up, face the struggle and live somewhere the sun never stopped shining.

The door opened and JCO Brown told Rude, "You're off lockdown, you can come out now."

Rude slowly rose from the bed and buttoned his jumpsuit, then went to wash his face and brush his teeth in the sink in his room while he looked out the cracked door down at the dorm below. Rude turned, rinsed his mouth out, spit in the toilet and flushed it. When he turned back around, Pistol was standing at the door looking out at the dorm as if posted on guard.

"Fuck going on, bruh?" Rude said as he walked out of the door and clasped Pistol's hands in a brotherly shake. Both leaned on the rail of the top range and looked at the dorm below.

"I thought they was never gonna let us up out them rooms," Pistol said.

"Man fuck these folks. If somebody else get smart out the mouth, I'ma smash the gas on they ass," Rude swore as his eyes found Penny who was in a heated discussion with some big black kid.

Rude could tell by how the two were raising their hands frantically, clearly trying to get a point across. Rude looked at the JCO who was sitting at the desk with his feet kicked up laughing into the phone at the desk.

"Ain't that lil' bruh you in the room with?" Pistol asked as he too soon picked up the scene that was unfolding.

"Hell yeah," Rude stated trying to see if Penny was all talk or about all that shit he had been talking.

The big dude suddenly pointed toward the shower on the bottom range and Penny immediately followed him.

"They 'bout to go hit," Pistol spoke peeping the movement also his eyes on the other two young niggas who were clearly with the big black one as they eyed Penny with evil intentions in their eyes.

"Fuck them hoe ass niggas gon' do?" Rude huffed catching the other two boys staring at Penny as he walked by.

Rude immediately made his way to the stairs and began to descend them until he was in the dayroom and positioned himself where he could watch Penny as he headed down the stairs. Penny hadn't even made it to the first step before he pulled out a white sack filled with something and began swinging the sack rapidly, each blow catching the big black dude on the head, splitting him on contact as he fell down the rest of the stairs onto the floor as the kids began to shout, "Fight! Fight! Fight!"

Rude peeped the two boys making their way over to the stairs and ran over to them, knocking kids out the way with Pistol right on his heels. Rude caught the last one as he was about to take a step down the stairs and hit him with a vicious blow to the back of the head that sent him sprawling down the stairs into the other boy making him fall onto the cement floor lip busting from the contact his face made with stairs and began stomping the big dude as Penny turned and began hitting the other boys with the bloodied sack that he had clenched in his hand.

Rude hopped onto one of the fallen boys and began beating him mercilessly taking out his pent-up rage on the face of the boy.

"Police! Police!" the youth shouted but the three refused to stop the assault as they beat the boys to unrecognizable states.

The first one to go down was Penny as they slammed him onto his side causing him to shriek, "Ahhh!"

Rude turned to the cry of his fallen comrade as hopped off the boy and ran over to the two officers who had Penny pinned down and swung on the first officer his fist could reach.

Smack! Sounded the impact of Rude's fist as it collided with the small JCO's face knocking him down, but before Rude could turn to the officer, he was tackled from behind.

"Ahhh!" Rude moaned as he hit the concrete face first with his hands cut breaking the fall.

After the JCOs had gained control of the situation and had removed the beaten and bloody victims from the area they got orders from Lieutenant McDail to take Penny, Rude and Pistol to isolation and for them to remain there until further notice. The trio thanked him by shouting a bunch of obscenities that hit him in the back, but he never turned around to acknowledge them.

****

It had been six months since that incident and the three grew even closer as they did their time together in isolation. Rude had gone to juvenile court and was sentenced to one-hundred and twenty days and his time was up. He promised his newly acquainted brothers over and over they would meet up again in the future and make the ground shake.

"Bruh, y'all niggas stay solid and come onto the streets we got shit we tryna do," Rude stated from up under the door of his cell.

"Bruh, you already know I'ma see you in about ninety days," Pistol replied from under the door.

"You alright, Pennywise?" Rude asked knowing Penny had grown attached to him and would be the most affected by his departure.

"I'm good, bruh, just can't wait to get up out of here," Penny said the sadness could be heard in his words.

"Bruh, stay the fuck out of trouble. You ain't got but sixty more days," Rude advised.

"Time for you to go, Mr. Preston," JCO Mason said as she licked her thick lip gloss coated lips at Rude.

JCO Mason was a thick, peach-skinned toned woman who was rumored to be an ex-stripper. She was 5'2, 135 pounds, and had an ass that could stop traffic. JCO Mason liked Rude, they had been swapping letters back and forth since she had been posted to work the isolation pad the three were housed in. Rude took advantage of the occasion to plant a seed he had been wanting to plant, but due to the eyes of the officers and juveniles in the regular dorm, he never got a chance.

"Let's go," Rude stated as he stood at the door of the cell ready to get up out of there.

JCO Mason opened the door and Rude dragged his belongings out of the cell. Dropping them on the floor, he took two bags that were filled with snacks, walked over to Pistol's cell and opened the tray flap, then pushed the bag through the flap and dropped two weed sticks rolled up in tissue in his lap. He shook his hand, then repeated the process with Pennywise.

"Don't forget your paperwork," JCO Mason spoke pointing at the chair where she sat when she walked the pod.

Rude looked at the paper and back toward JCO Mason who had her hand up in the shape of a phone letting Rude know what time it was. Rude picked up the paper and folded it, then put it in the front pocket of his blue jumpsuit with a smile on his face knowing he had accomplished his mission. Rude looked around to see if anybody was looking and walked over to JCO Mason who had walked into his room inspecting his cell making sure he hadn't left anything in the room. Rude walked up behind her and pressed his dick into her back causing her to gasp in shock.

"Boy, you gon' get me fired," JCO Mason moaned as Rude sucked softly on her neck.

Rude, knowing he had to break loose before he got her in trouble, stepped back out the cell and just as he did Lieutenant Mango had rounded the corner.

'*Close call*,' Rude thought as he peeped Lieutenant Mango heading their way with his black beady eyes sweeping the area.

Lieutenant Mango was a big, black, sloppy dude who was always trying to block the young niggas from hollering at the female guards because he was too busy trying to buy pussy himself. "Preston, you ready?" Lieutenant Mango asked watching JCO Mason, drinking in her every curve as she bent over cleaning the toilet of Rude's vacated cell.

'*Perverted ass, nigga*,' Rude thought before saying, "Yeah, I'm ready to go." He began walking out into the sally port, leaving Lieutenant Mango trying to get something he already had.

Several minutes later, Lieutenant Mango walked out the pad with a defeated look on his face and JCO Mason on his heels.

Once she saw Rude, she smiled her infamous smile and said, "Stay out of trouble. I know you got somebody out there that cares about you."

"Something like that," Rude shot as he watched JCO Mason blow him a kiss with her juicy lips when she peeped Lieutenant Mango wasn't paying attention.

"Let's go, Preston," Mango said walking him to the door of the sally port that led to the white-tiled hallway, leading to the front of the detention center.

Rude walked through the door and began striding up the long hallways until he came upon an intersection, turned left, walked around main-control, walked toward intake and went through the door that led to where his stay at the detention had started.

Lieutenant Mango walked to the back and Rude began stripping out the state clothes. JCO Payne walked through the door Lieutenant Mango had walked into with Rude's clothes in a blue bag and said, "Here," with a scowl on his face.

Rude snatched the bag and dared Payne to say something that would provoke him to get on his ass, but Payne said nothing and hurriedly went back through the door he came out of.

Rude looked into the bag at his soiled clothes and didn't want to put the blood-soaked clothes on again, too many bad memories rushing him. But he had no choice, so he put the shorts, shirt, and shoes on and left the rest except his brother's old phone in there. Lieutenant Mango walked back out of the room and handed Rude some papers to sign. Rude signed them briskly, then walked around the corner to the front of the intake area and up to the door that was holding him from freedom. Walking up to the door and peering out, Rude saw something that nearly made his eyes pop out.

Stacey was standing with a swollen belly next to a police officer, clearly about to get booked in. Rude couldn't make out what was being said between the officer and Ms. Zone 3, the tears that ran freely down Stacey's beautiful face spoke volumes, but they didn't move Rude. He felt no remorse for her as his blood boiled and murder danced in his mind as their last encountered played back in his head. Feeling his eyes on her, Stacey turned her head toward the direction she felt the energy coming from and her breath caught in her chest as she thought she was seeing a ghost.

'My baby's daddy!' Stacey thought badly wanting to scream out to Rude and let him know about the baby in her stomach and how much she had been going through since they had last seen each other, but too scared to speak.

Stacey wiped the tears out of her eyes and tried to smile, but it didn't work as more tears slid down her face.

Rude dropped his head, dreads falling in his face as emotions coursed through his body from the buried feeling he had for Stacey.

"Lorenzo!" Stacey began screaming, but Rude ignored her and backed away from the door out of her sight.

Her voice was still shattering the quietness of the area, but Rude blocked her out of his head and would continue to do for the rest of his life, until the time was right for her to pay the debt she owed to him, something he promised himself, her and Kissy Pooh would pay regardless of the circumstances.

Chapter 6

At first sight of his mother, Rude knew she had fallen back into the shell of her old self. Her temper constantly flared and her hair was just thrown into a ponytail. Her clothes were dirty and dingy and when he took his first step into the house, the stench it possessed from neglect was so powerful he had to step back out of the house to gather himself before he went back in. After assessing the situation, Rude began to clean the house like an obedient son would do despite his mother not once thanking him for the deed, but his purpose wasn't to gain thanks it was to keep the peace between them. Something he so badly wanted ever since his big brother died. He understood on another level that he could be next, he only had one mother, so he wanted to make shit right.

Day after day his mother smoked her life away and the bills continued to pile up. First, the lights went out in the house, Rude went and confronted his mother only to find her room candlelit and her lost in a drug-induced nod. He then turned on his heels and left her there. The water went next, Rude lost his temper, spazzed out on his mother and beat her boyfriend up when he tried to push up and take up for his mother. His mother immediately rushed to her boyfriend's aid and jumped on Rude with her boyfriend.

Rude never let up as she scratched him and beat on his back. Only when he felt the body beneath cease to move did he turn his attention to his mother and pushed her up against the wall.

He looked into her reddened eyes with tears running down his face and said, "Come on, mama. I tried to be a good son and look what you've become. I'm not gonna sit here and watch you decay and destroy your life. I'm gonna gon' head and leave." Rude then let her go and walked toward his room, but before he stepped into his room, he turned back to his mother rushing toward her fallen boyfriend.

Rude turned back toward his room, head hanging, and went to pack his things. Then he left out the door and his mother's life forever into the streets where he knew he would find what his heart desired and what would wash his memory of his mother out his mind, or so he thought. Rude had refused going to school after the first two weeks seeing that it didn't benefit his immediate future. Miracle was hurt by the sudden change in Rude but swore to be there for him. Rude told her simply she wasn't ready for his lifestyle and left her in tears as he turned and walked out of the school, closing another chapter in his life.

Rude had been staying at Moe's spot for a couple of weeks building a relationship with JCO Mason who he now referred to as Tameka. Today was the first day they were supposed to meet up. Rude was hoping to solidify some shit so he could finally find him a place to stay other than Moe's spot. He was getting irritated more and more from waking to find bad ass kids running, screaming and crying all the time. Even though he had love for them, he still felt he had to gone head and find a better place and a way to start touching some paper because he couldn't eat air and his car couldn't either. Today was the day he was finally supposed to meet up with Tameka to go on what she termed their first date, but Rude wasn't thinking about that, his only thoughts was a way to make it where he could slide up under her and control her mind.

Rude stood outside dressed in black Polo boots, Akademik jeans, a black T-shirt, a black and brown fur rimmed Polo jacket, and a black A-town fitted cap with earmuffs on it smoking a blunt with Bozo, Wise-Guy, and Dubb. The three had recently been hanging around Moe's spot since Rude had been released from juvenile. Bozo was from Hollywood, Florida and was notorious for being a stick-up kid. He was dark-skinned, slightly muscled, and stood 5'8. He also had a mouth full of 24 kt. gold something all niggas from Florida chose to wear. Bozo really didn't stay in one place for too long and moved around in his gold Chevy Caprice. Bozo had been on his own since his parents had in a fire while he was at school at the age of ten. So, he was forced to grow up in foster home after foster home until he eventually grew tired of that and turned to the streets.

Wise-Guy was a young nigga barely twenty from Washington circle in East Point, GA. He was a tall, lanky, brown-skinned dude with dreads that hung to his shoulders. Wise-Guy was the oldest out of seven kids his mother had birthed into the world. Like all young niggas with no father, he too turned to the streets and they filled the void his father left by catching a life-sentence back in the eighties for trafficking bricks of heroin. Wise-Guy got his name from the slick way he moved in the streets that enable him to always come out on top whether it was finessing a hoe out of something or finessing a nigga out of the sack. Basically, if he saw a way to profit, he made sure his goal was met. He took as less a risk as possible by keeping his nose clean. Not many trusted him because of word in the streets declaring him a snake-ass-nigga for the check.

Dubb was an older dude who stayed with his parents who always seemed to know where the best parties and licks were, so he was valuable to any nigga that was looking to strike in the streets. Dubb wore his long hair in plaits and golds in his mouth to disguise his fucked-up grill. He was also from East Point, the young niggas looked up to him like a big brother out there. Dubb drove an old school sky blue two-door Cadillac with 24-inch rims that squeaked as it moved through the streets from the rims scratching the fender of the car. If only one of them was cutthroat, then it would have been Dubb who was known in the streets for crossing niggas and laughing 'bout it when confronted like it was a joke. Dubb was twenty-seven and had no future, his only goal was to be able to buy a new outfit and hit the club every week.

Just the week before he had gotten Wise-Guy to break in Bozo's car and steal three pounds of weed and about $1500 in cash. Everything Bozo had to his name, so he was back on the fuck shit and even as they stood there huddled in the cold, passing blunts around he was stressing that shit while eyeing Dubb and Wise-Guy suspiciously thinking thoughts of murder if he found out they were the ones who'd gone in his shit.

"Fuck niggas stole everything. Then to make shit even worse, they poured sugar in a nigga gas tank. Some shit a hoe would do," Bozo stated before taking a toke of the blunt he had in his hands.

"No!" Dubb said with an expression indicating disbelief on his face, but the whole time saying in his head, '*Sweet ass, nigga.*'

"Damn, bruh," Rude said before taking the blunt while eyeing Dubb who he'd gotten a bad vibe off of from the jump.

There was just something about the half-smiles that always seemed to creep across his face, that made Rude distrust him and little did he know, his intuition was on point. Because Dubb was forever on the bullshit and played to win with no regard for anybody but himself.

"Who the fuck that is?" Wise-Guy asked as he watched the cocaine white 2009 Dodge Challenger come to a stop in front of Moe's lawn.

Rude looked toward the car and knew it was Tameka, so he stood there finishing the blunt as she strode up the driveway, hips swaying gracefully making the niggas around him make sexual comments about what they would do to her.

Tameka, seeing Rude, walked up to him and placed her arms around his neck, while Rude gripped her juicy ass as he gave her a peck on her forever glossy lips. Rude leaned in and told her to go wait for him in the car. Tameka obliged and turned after saying bye to the niggas surrounding Rude smoking.

Wise-Guy was the first to speak as he watched Tameka's ass bounce as she headed back down the driveway. "Boy, you done caught one." He was thinking if he was ever given the chance, he would pull up on shawty.

"Somethin' like that, but I'ma fuck with y'all niggas later," Rude replied giving them daps.

Dubb stopped him before he left and asked, "You still tryna make some money?" He started pulling on the Newport he had just lit.

"Fuckin' right!" Rude answered wondering what type of move Dubb was trying to make.

"Well, holla at me when you get through fucking with shawty."

"Say no more," Rude agreed, then turned to leave thinking he might have come to judgment too quick about Dubb. He might be a good nigga after all, but he still would let time speak for that, because like his brother always told him a nigga would change up on you in the blink of an eye if the price was right or his future depended upon giving up or doing the time.

****

"So, you really tryna make shit work between us?" Rude asked as he toyed with the sirloin steak on his plate, staring into Tameka's eyes at the table.

She was eating shrimp, making it look like the sexiest thing in the world, sucking the shrimp softly before swallowing it as she stared at Rude enticingly. The two sat at a table in the infamous Benny Hanna's restaurant in Atlantic Station, an upscale part of the Atlanta area.

"I wouldn't have slid you my number if I didn't want to make something out of this. Besides, I see something in you that draws me near. It makes me want to better understand your life's struggle," Tameka replied as she picked up the glass of Sprite and took a sip.

Tameka was from the West End, an area in the city where corruption prevailed over kindness. After years of struggling, the streets had been somewhat good to her family, and she made it to the point of independence. She didn't like school very much, so she dropped out and started stripping while earning her G.E.D. at night. Her mother didn't approve and didn't have much control, because once Tameka saw that it was a problem, she immediately moved out after having saved a few months of income from stripping at Club Onyx. The club life had brought her face to face with the rawness of the streets and opened her eyes to levels of the street that she didn't even know existed. Through her experiences in the streets, she gained the smarts they offered, but the lifestyle quickly grew old, as rapes began to occur more often. The situation that struck the most was her friend Star, who had gotten killed in a shoot-out that erupted in the strip-club one night between two rival crews.

After that, it was never the same for her, so at twenty-five, she made the decision to strive for more out of life then what the streets had to offer. She knew life was unpredictable and tomorrow could be your last tomorrow. She wanted to have kids, a house and a husband to be there whenever she came home to rub her feet while asking how her day was, and things of that nature. Because out of all the things she'd been taught by her father before he passed away after getting killed in the streets over some drug beef, was how a man should treat his woman and vice versa. Tameka was still looking as she sat at the table across from Rude, she felt she had just started walking down the right path.

"You right, I'm not gon' lie, that shit was a surprise for a minute. I thought you were blind to the fact that the truth was standing in your face."

"Nigga please!" Tameka replied, rolling her eyes sexily as she stuck another shrimp into her juicy lips taking a small bite.

"I'm on some more shit, though. I don't need no temporary. I don't want no secrets. I need a full time, or I don't need you at all," Rude said thinking of all the women he had in his life before his brother's death, how simple minded they were and how that was something he wasn't going to tolerate.

"I'm ready for whatever you can handle," Tameka shot back, staring into Rude's eyes letting him know she meant what she was saying. "Say no more," Tameka said as she grabbed her cream-colored Chanel purse off the table, opened it and pulled out a small roll of bills, dropping them on the table.

"So, where we headed now?" Rude asked his mind now on the conversation he was supposed to be having with Dubb about a score. Something he needs bad because he was dead broke and wasn't with that free-loading shit.

"You already know where we headed."

"And where's that?" Rude asked, then kissed Tameka on the forehead as they pushed through the entrance door back into the cold starless night.

"To seal the deal," Tameka stated ready to see if Rude had the tools to bag up the shit he was kicking cause a man with no dick game was a man she didn't need.

Chapter 7

Rude, Bozo, Wise-Guy, and Dubb were sitting in Bozo's Caprice passing a blunt around under the gloomy day of Christmas Eve plotting on a robbery.

"You almost didn't make it because Peewee and them almost fucked up the move," stated Dubb as he twisted a blunt of hydro that he had recently purchased.

Peewee was a young nigga from East Point who Dub had brought in . "They froze up on some scary shit, but I already know you gon' go and that's why we here," Dubb stated as he sipped on a Bud Lite, staring outside at a young girl who was walking past with some tight grey jogging pants on and her ass bouncing every way. '*Gotta pull up on shawty later if everything go through,*' Dubb thought.

"I appreciate that. So, what we 'bout to strike on?" Rude asked, butterflies in his stomach because of this being his first robbery.

"Lil nigga, we just want you to grab all the money while we do the rest," Wise commanded putting bullets into the clip of the High Point .45 Caliber handgun he had.

Dubb had been working at the Family Dollar in Tri-city Plaza for a little over a month now, he felt the time was right for them to pull a caper. Dubb hopped from store to store setting them up after becoming familiar with the schedules, rotations, and the days when the safe had accumulated over $7,000 and Dubb knew this.

"All I want y'all to do is go to the back of the store, slide through the employee's only area and hide behind all the boxes that will be scattered back there, preferably the dock area until I give you a call letting you know the store has closed. Around that time, they should be in the back with the safe open, counting the money. Tonight is the night they take the money to the bank. So, you gotta make this shit count and the most crucial thing is to make sure y'all get the tape," Dubb schooled over what he felt was a fool-proof plan.

"Sweet!" Wise exclaimed as he handed the .45 to Rude.

Rude took the gun and stared at it, awestruck at the size of the gun being that it was his second time actually holding one.

"That's what I told them nigga's the first time, but look what happened," Dubb said with annoyance in his voice from the thoughts of Pee Wee, Spoke, and Duck fucking up the move.

"Y'all niggas ready?" Bozo asked who hadn't said much since they'd been in the car.

Bozo was getting bad vibes off Dubb. Every time he looked over to the passenger side, something inside him told him Dubb had something to do with his shit being stolen. But Bozo wasn't about to let that come between what they were about to do that night.

Snow had just begun to fall, blanketing the ground with white, something that was uncommon in the Atlanta and Metro areas but had been occurring more regularly in the last two years.

"It's snowing, this is the perfect time!" Dubb stated, feeling good about tonight, knowing in two hours he should be ducked off somewhere with Keisha. The girl who had walked past the car earlier in the grey sweatpants getting his dick sucked, while smoking a fat blunt.

"Let's get it, bruh, gone pull off," Dubb stated, finally easing the tension in the car from the anticipation of the lick.

Dubb pulled the blunt one more time before passing it to Bozo. Bozo took the blunt, pulled out of Moe's driveway and smashed the gas with thoughts of lick money on his mind.

****

The store was crowded with customers who were looking to buy late Christmas gifts, filling the air with the feeling only the holiday season could. No one paid attention to the three heavily clothed men as they came through the door four minutes apart from each other because everybody's thoughts were on making it back to their loved ones to enjoy the special day that only happened one time a year.

Rude walked down an aisle separate from Bozo and Wise, blending in with the shoppers looking no one in the face as he scanned the shelves as if looking for things to purchase. Making his way to the back of the store on the aisle that they sold washing powders and detergent. Rude spotted Wise slide through the employees only door swiftly. Sweat trickled down Rude's back even though the store wasn't even hot, but the nervousness that permeated through his body was causing the heat to course through his body.

'Now or never,' Rude thought as he watched an old white lady who was the last person on the aisle who could be a witness to him going through the door, turn on another aisle. Rude took another glance around the area before he opened the door and slipped through silently. Moving through the numerous stacked boxes, Rude made his way to the back of the store, until he reached the loading area and walked around crates filled with boxes until he could no further. That is where he found Bozo who he hadn't seen come through the door and Wise sitting down with their backs pressed against some boxes, both had a .45 handgun a piece in their hands with expressionless faces.

Rude took his spot next to Wise, then closed his eyes and began counting to a thousand, trying not to think about the present situation and what would happen if they were caught back there. It seemed like days that they had been back there to Rude, but it had only been a few hours. Just when he thought he was gonna lose his mind, he heard the vibration from Bozo's phone go off. Rude looked over at Bozo who was texting back swiftly.

Bozo finished, looked up and whispered, "Bruh, said they cut the lights off in the front."

They all knew that was the signal letting them know the front door of the store was locked, and workers should be in the back with the safe open counting the money. Wise rose and did a quick stretch without a word, then pulled the ski-mask down over his face. Bozo didn't have one, so he pulled the fitted cap down low on his head and Rude threw the hood of his black pullover atop his head and followed Bozo and Wise as they silently crept back around in the direction they had come from. Wise turned and put his finger to his lips as he heard sounds of conversation, then the unmistakable sound of coins clinking.

"Damn, Tyrone, I never knew Family Dollar would be docking this much money," a female voice spoke, clearly new to the store.

"Yeah, we have our days," a man sounded with a deep baritone voice.

"I can't wait to get home—" The female's words were cut short when she saw the ski-masked man appear from around a stack of boxes with a gun in his hand.

"Ahhh!" the female screamed her eyes wide as saucers as she frantically pointed toward the robber.

Fuk Shyt

"Bitch shut the fuck up!" Wise yelled pointing the .45 at a light-skinned, tall, dread-headed man who was standing beside her placing the money in the safe.

"Take it, all you can—" *Whap!* Wise slammed the pistol across the heavy-set female's head causing a river of blood to pour down her face.

Bozo and Rude wasted no time seeing that the situation was under control. Bozo went to the recording monitor and ejected the tape, as Rude grabbed a bag and started racking stack after stack into it as well as coins that were in stacks, then he turned to the register on the table that the female sat at bleeding and started stuffing that money in the bag also.

"Done?" Wise asked as he trained the pistol on the light-skinned dread head.

"Yeah!" Rude shouted as he backpedaled out of the office with the money in his hand.

Whap! Whap! Whap! Wise struck the guy in the head repeatedly until his body dropped to the floor. The heavyset female was shaking from fear and jumped when Wise shouted, "Bitch, get under the table!" Seeing her get under the table, Wise laughed menacingly, then turned and ran past Bozo and Rude kicking boxes until he reached the emergency door in the back of the store.

Wasting no time, Wise hopped down onto the pavement and ran toward the car Dubb had brought around the back waiting on them to come out. Rude ran behind Bozo, jumped off the platform onto the ground and made it to the Caprice, then jumped in the backseat, slamming the door as Dubb merked off into the night, sealing the deal on their getaway.

****

"So how much we got?" Bozo asked while looking in the backseat of the car at Wise and Rude continuously on point for any bullshit knowing Wise and Dubb be on some cut-throat shit.

"We got a lil over eleven gees," Rude said, counting the last stack of crumpled dollar bills before placing them on the seat with the rest of the stacks him and Wise had counted out.

"Damn, that mothafucka was strapped. I might need to hit me some more of them!" Bozo stated wondering how many he would have to hit before he saw a hundred thousand.

"Fuckin' right," Rude added, never having seen that much money at one time in his life.

The feeling of having money was something that made him feel like he was on top of the world, like he couldn't be told no, or treated like he wasn't shit. Something he felt deep down within him could be a part of him for the rest of his life because, in that short time, he knew he didn't want to live without it. Money was power and power was the ability to change.

"Look, give me four grand and y'all split the rest," Dubb stated out of nowhere as he sat with his feet on the ground outside the car, blowing cigarette smoke into the air, as he stared at the light drizzle of snowfall on the ground.

They were in a neighborhood next door to 'New Landings' called Forest Downs in a cul-de-sac in the back of the quiet neighborhood.

"Bruh, you got me fucked up!" Wise screamed, immediately angered by the statement Dubb had made. "Nigga, you didn't even go in the store! What the fuck make you think you can call that order, nigga?" Wise stared at Dubb who kept looking into the night.

Dubb turned his head, blew smoke in Wise's direction and said, "Nigga, I'm the one who turned y'all onto the lick. Besides nigga when you started kicking tough shit? You must wanna get one or something?" Dubb replied with even more aggression in his words.

"Fuck nigga, you ain't said shit!" Wise answered opening the rear door and walking around the car.

Dubb stood also, dropped the half-smoked cigarette on the ground and braced himself for the fight. "Fuck nigga?" Dubb insulted before hawking and spitting on Wise.

Wise stepped back out of surprise and wiped the spit off his face. Dubb rushed him and swung a left hook. Wise ducked, pushed Dubb away from him, whipped out the pistol he had tucked in the front of his hoodie and pointed it at Dubb who froze immediately at the sight. Time seemed to stop as everybody's eyes locked on Wise as he walked up on Dubb with the pistol leveled at his head.

"Fuck nigga, you a hoe, do somethin' now pussy!" Wise spat knowing he had the upper hand in the situation.

"Damn, Wise, that shit ain't that serious," Bozo said trying to mediate the situation before it turned to a deadly ending.

Wise ignored him and spit in Dubb's face who still didn't move as the spit ran down his face. Dubb eyed Wise with nothing but fear in his heart, not from Wise himself, but the gun and how it possessed the power to end his life. He knew you didn't have to be built like that to pull a trigger a sucker killed a real nigga every day in the streets.

"Nigga, fuck this guy, I ain't in the mood to spare shit!" Wise screamed, face balled up in rage as he pulled the trigger, sending a bullet through Dubb's head which knocked off a small portion as he dropped to the ground soundlessly, with the snow breaking the fall.

Porch lights immediately started lighting the porches, driveway lights lit the paths of the driveways and dogs started barking, disturbed by the sound of gunfire.

"Oh, shit!" Rude exclaimed, watching blood leak out of the bullet wound in Dubb's lifeless body as it twitched and convulsed.

Wise turned to the Caprice as Bozo and Rude sat in it quietly. He smiled and said, "Wow, look at this bitch. He ain't poppin' that tough shit now," Then he walked up and emptied the rest of the clip in Dubb's body, his body jerked from the impact of every shot.

"Bruh, let's go, that nigga dead!" Bozo screamed, cranking the Caprice up ready to depart the murder scene.

Wise-Guy looked down at Dubb's lifeless body one more time, then kicked it before he ran to the car and hopped in the passenger seat as Bozo floored the gas pedal, fleeing the scene.

Chapter 8

"Bruh, I gotta drop this money off at Ma Dukes. Then we gon' hit D.O.A. and see what you talking 'bout," Rude stated as he turned into the New Landings subdivision in his brother's old Cutlass that he had just gotten repainted a glossy black, added a new sound system, and 21% tint on the windows.

"Bruh, I'm telling you, these hoes gon' be in there. Plus, my partner Day-Day big brother work security at the door. So, we just gon' pay a lil' extra and we in there," Pistol replied who had just been released from Metro YDC a few weeks ago.

Rude made the first move of loyalty and had a few outfits and a couple of hundred dollars waiting on him when he got out. This didn't surprise Pistol, he already knew what type of nigga he was dealing with.

"Bruh, who that hoe?" Pistol asked looking at a thick, light-skinned female walking up a driveway surrounded by three children carrying groceries.

"Oh, that ain't shit, right there. Shawty got more children than a foster home, you' on want that. She don' burned three niggas in the last two months," Rude answered, he himself almost fell victim to Pauline's allure.

"Damn, bruh, these hoes ain't shit," Pistol commented, leaning back in the seat.

Rude slowed the car down as they neared his house and immediately became paranoid from seeing all the police cars and ambulance in front of his house.

"What the fuck going on up here?" Pistol questioned out of impulse, reaching to hide something then realizing he didn't have anything.

"That's my spot they at, bruh. Look, stay here, I gotta find out what's going on," Rude said putting the car in park, then hopping out.

Rude's heart thumped wildly in his chest as he watched the paramedics wheel a gurney out of his house. A group of policemen stood in the driveway congregating as Rude walked up. Rude looked around and saw his neighbors on their porches, so he walked toward the house on the right of his where Ms. Jackson lived alone with her daughter Destiny who he had fucked a couple of times since he'd been staying in the neighborhood. Destiny was on the porch with her mother, as soon as she saw Rude, she burst into tears and ran toward him.

Rude caught her in his arms and asked her while trying to soothe her, "What's going on?"

Destiny looked up through tears and said, "Your mother was killed by her boyfriend."

Rude unwrapped his arms from around her then turned toward his driveway and started running toward his home. Rude made it to the door just as they were bringing a second gurney out of the house. He ran up to the group of policemen who immediately turned toward him but only one said something.

That was Officer Carmichael who knew Rude personally from his many run-ins with the Fulton County Police Department. "Listen, son," Officer Carmichael said, putting his hand up to slow Rude down.

"Nah, fuck that! What happened?" Rude bellowed as tears ran down his face from the fear of losing the last person on Earth he truly had and loved, despite everything his mother had taken him through. She had never abandoned him when he was born, so he was grateful for that because a lot of people he knew didn't even know their parents.

The officers standing in the driveway tensed up at the loudness of Rude's words, but Officer Carmichael waved a hand to calm them, then turned toward Rude again and said, "Your mother was killed, then the man we assume was her spouse killed himself."

Before the last words were out of his mouth Rude had dropped to his knees with his head in his hands and despair in his heart, wondering if there really was a God and why he was taking so much out of his life.

"Son, everything is going to be alright," Officer Carmichael said placing a hand on Rude's shoulder.

"Get yo' muhfuckin' hands off me!" Rude screamed shaking the officer's hand off him then standing and turning, heading back towards the car.

"Lorenzo!" Destiny and her mother shouted.

Rude ignored them as he got into the Cutlass and smashed off with the fuck shit on his mind.

****

"Bruh, I want a nigga head now, I don't give a fuck. The first nigga I see gon' get it," Rude said as he lurked through the streets looking for a target with Pistol on the passenger side.

"Bruh, since we going in, we might as well make that shit count," Pistol stated not wanting to crash out on no humbug shit.

"You right, I got the perfect shit in mind," Rude replied whipping the car around and smashing up a hill in the New Landings subdivision, headed toward the neighborhood weed man Dino who Rude had spared on the strength of Rod and the Been 'Bout A Check clique Dino was part of. But how the tables had turned, Rude was about to wipe his nose clean. Rude stopped in front of Dino's house and spotted Dino's 1976 white Chevelle sitting in the driveway.

'*That nigga alone,*' Rude thought as he jumped out of the car, slamming the door. "Shawty the weed man pushing about four or five bags, maybe more," Rude informed as Pistol trailed him, looking from side to side trying to see if they were being watched not knowing how Rude was about to pull this shit off being that they didn't even have a pistol.

The door opened before they even made it to the door, Dino stepped out with no shirt on, his fat stomach jiggling and with a 9 mm in his hand.

"What's up, big bruh," Rude said sounding casual not wanting to shake Dino up, knowing how scary the California nigga was.

"Shit, my nigga, what's going on? Come on in and let me blow ya head off. I just got this new pack in from Cali," Dino answered stepping aside, letting Rude and Pistol through.

"Who bruh?" Dino asked with suspicion in his eyes from the new face.

"Oh, this my partner, I met in juvy named Pistol. He wanted to buy a QP," Rude answered as they walked to the living room, that was decked out in black leather with a large flat screen television playing *Paid in Full*. The air smelled of a strong pungent weed aroma, letting Rude and Pistol know off the dribble that the pack was in there.

"Oh, shit bruh, that shit dumb loud," Rude stated plopping down in the black, soft, leather armchair.

"Baby, you got visitors?" a thick, dark-skinned woman asked, standing in the kitchen butt naked, drinking orange juice.

"Yeah, gon' head upstairs and put some clothes on." Dino slapped her on the ass as she walked by making her soft ass jiggle, giving Pistol and Rude a good view.

"That's a grown woman, right there. Y'all young niggas wouldn't know what to do with that," Dino stated as he walked over to the mini bar in the corner of the living room, sat the pistol on the table and picked up a jar filled with weed.

"This that Irene, right here. Three-fifty a zip, the best shit smoking in the city," Dino bragged, unscrewing the lid off the jar and handing it to Pistol who was standing next to the arm-chair Rude was sitting in. Pistol took the jar and inhaled the pungent aroma deeply, never before having smelled weed so strong. "Since I fuck with, lil bruh, I'ma smoke one on the strength," Dino stated as he took the jar back and shook a bud in his hand.

Dino turned and that was the worst thing he could have done because immediately Pistol threw his thick muscled arm around his neck and put him in a chokehold. As Rude jumped out of the armchair, reached for the pistol on the bar and slammed the butt of the pistol down on Dino's head, ceasing the struggle he was taking Pistol through, knocking him out cold.

"Oh, my God!" the dark-skinned woman screamed, she'd just walked back into the room with a silk robe wrapped around her body.

"Bitch don't move!" Rude shouted with ice in his voice as he pointed the pistol at her.

Rude stood and made four strides across the room then yanked the woman by her head toward where Dino was sprawled unconsciously on the floor. Pistol then yanked the robe off the woman.

She put up no fight, but only kept whispering, "I know where everything is—just please don't rape me."

Pistol ripped the robe to shreds, then began tying Dino's legs and arms together tightly. As he did, Rude went into the kitchen and rumbled around in the drawers and cabinets until he found a trash bag, then came back and said, "Bruh, watch that fuck nigga and you come show me where everything at since you know so much."

The naked woman rose to her feet shaking, but she wasn't moving fast enough so Rude backhanded her causing her to crash into the black armchair and hit the floor.

"Bitch get the fuck up!" Rude shouted as he yanked the woman off the floor who now responded a lil' quicker as he dragged her off up the stairs.

"Aaahhh," Dino moaned as he started coming back into consciousness.

"Damn, fat boy, I thought yo' ass had died," Pistol joked now at the bar busting down a blunt about to fill it with some of the exotic weed in the jar on the table.

"Bruh, come on! This some fuck shit. Lil' bruh know I fuck with him. Why y'all doing me like this?" Dino asked with nothing but fear in his voice wishing he had never let the young nigga Rude in his house, knowing since he first started kicking it with Rod, he'd felt bad vibes from the young nigga.

"Cause we on that fuck shit!" Pistol shouted as he walked over to Dino and stood over him before pulling a Beretta .45 from behind his back and slamming the butt of the pistol back down on Dino's head, knocking him out cold once again.

****

"I always wondered what life would have been like if me and big bro's daddy would have been in our lives? How would things have turned out? Then I would look at you and how proud and independent you were and came to the conclusion that things probably wouldn't have been any different. You would've lived life how you wanted too regardless. There is just so much I never got to sit down and talk to you about. I guess I could blame that on me growing up too fast. I wish I could just go back in time and re-do a lot of the things I did that made you hate me so much. I used to try so hard to make you love me, but it seems like nothing worked." Rude wiped a tear out of his eye and stared into the bright sunny sky looking for a sign that his mother was looking down on him. "I don't know what I coulda did? Rod was against coming to you and you were against being a mother. The world is so messed up, I don't understand nothing but pain and the struggle." Rude looked at his mother's marble tombstone and wished it would talk back if only for this last time.

The funeral had ended for Rude's mother, he was the last one there. Rude was searching for answers and closure, something he never got while his mother was alive.

"I guess some things are unexplainable and you just have to deal with them whether you want to or not? But I've always looked at you at someone eternal, who was gonna be in my life forever. I guess, I was naïve and stuck in a childish mind-state, but you're my mama and it just don't feel right without you being here—damn," Rude mumbled as a new fresh set of tears tumbled down his face.

Rude sat down, put his back on his brother's black granite tombstone and stared into the distance at the sun as it began to set in the sky filling the sky with reddish orange.

How important it is to live stress-free and how it makes even the simplest things beautiful.

"Bruh, you already know how I'm rockin'. I don't even have to continue stressing this shit to you. I rather die than be a nobody—besides, fuck the world, it owes me everything," Rude stressed as he stared off into the horizon. "I got me a lil' bitch. Guess who? That lil' bitch from Metro Ms. Mason. Crazy, huh? Yeah, shawty came on in for the kid. So, you don't gotta worry about where I'ma rest my head. The streets still the same fuck nigga's telling, hoe's chasing sacks, and the regular shit. On some more shit though, I'm on the fuck shit and it's time the streets paid the piper. You already know, I'm about to get to Miami where we always dreamed of being when we retired from the streets."

Hearing footsteps, Rude looked back and was surprised to find Pistol and Pennywise walking his way. Rude stood and brushed grass off the black slacks he had on and said, "What's up?" He pulled Penny-wise in his arms and tussled his dreads.

"Shit bruh, we knew you would be out here, so we pulled up. You family and times like this are the ones when you need family around you," Pistol said sincerely as he stared Rude in the eyes.

"Already," Rude stated simply before giving Pistol a brotherly hug.

"Say 'round that's your brother's grave, right there?" Penny asked, pointing his head in the direction of the black tombstone.

"Hell yeah, that's bruh spot. He supposed to be here with us on the fuck shit," Rude answered with a sad smile on his face.

They all stood in silence studying Rod's grave before Pistol spoke, "Bruh, you already know we 'bout to carry the torch and make the ground shake 'round this motherfucka!"

"Fuckin' right, round! You already know I got somethin' on my chest," added Penny pulling out a blunt from his Tru Religion jeans, lighting it and pulling it three times before handing it to Rude.

"Yo' lil' badass don't care about shit, do you?" Rude said before pulling the potent weed, feeling the pain from the day leaving his body.

"Nigga, I'on see you putting that mu'fucka out," Pistol stated with a broad smile on his face.

Rude handed the blunt to him and said, "Nigga, shut up. How y'all get up here? I know Pistol broke ass ain't got no whip."

"Shit, we in a hotbox!" Penny replied with a nonchalant tone.

"Oh, y'all nigga's dumb hot. Let's get the fuck outta here before one of these old ass white folks call the police on us," Rude said causing Pistol and Penny to burst out laughing.

Chapter 9

"Bruh, this shit feel lame ass a mu'fucka," Pistol stated indicating Penny's idea of going door locking.

Penny bragged that he had struck on a couple of capers door locking. How he knew a couple of niggas who had a crew that specialized in the hustle, who had found half a million in the trunk of an old school. Even then Pistol kept his doubts, but Rude was down with whatever. To him, it was just another day to come up on a sack. Tonight, they were in *Magic City's* parking lot on the *Infamous Magic City Monday* and what some may have called street royalty were out, including the usual athletes, rappers, and stars that filled the city. The parking lot was filled with so many cars it was impossible for security to guard them all. This is why Penny chose tonight to veil their intentions.

The three had been sitting in a rented Red 2010 Dodge Challenger, smoking blunts and waiting on the crowd in the parking lot to dwindle before they made their move.

"Bruh, I'm telling you we gon' catch tonight round. Why you keep tripping? I know what it is you wanna go inside so you can trick off? My question is how you gon' get in and you broke nigga?" Penny stated then curled up laughing in the backseat.

"Nigga fuck you!" Pistol shot back with a smirk on his face.

"Say, lil bruh, it's time to make a move we ain't got all night. It's already eleven thirty," Rude said, ready to go ahead and get the move over with hoping the shit paid off because they were running low on funds. They didn't even have any guns so it was no way they could pull bigger moves.

"Say no more, big bruh. I'ma show y'all niggas how this shit done," Penny schooled unwrapping the brown extension cord he had just picked up off the seat. Penny got out of the car and waited for Rude and Pistol.

"Say round, y'all niggas taking too long," Penny muttered, already having his eyes on a choice whip.

No longer in the mood for small talk, Rude asked, "Which one?" As he looked around the large parking lot at all the cars, SUVs, and trucks.

"See the trick is to get the least expected one—not the Maserati's, Porches, and all of that other bullshit," Penny schooled walking up to a Black Denali truck.

"What the fuck? Why you ain't choose the Infinity truck or something else? You know a nigga dropped the check on it. You chose the cheapest mu'fucking whip in the parking lot," Pistol stated, clearly annoyed by Penny's actions.

Ignoring Pistol, Penny cocked his arm back and brought the extension cord plug down on the driver's side window, shattering it without a sound.

"Oooh, that's why you got that shit. Yo lil' ass a professional thief," Rude joked as he looked around making sure no one was approaching.

Pennywise opened the passenger door, hit all the locks, opening all the doors, then went up under the seat of the driver's side and groped around until his hands felt the cold metal.

Penny pulled the cold metal from under the seat which was a Browning 9mm handgun and shouted, "Bingo!" He started waving the pistol for his brothers to see.

Rude and Pistol's faces lit up forcing them to abandon their posts as lookouts and they began searching the truck. Rude got up in the truck, climbed to the back and found a black bag with stacks of crisp bills in it, also what looked like a clown mask and shouted, "Got cash!" Then he held up the bag.

Rude popped the center console and pulled out another gun which was a plastic Glock .40. Pistol had opened the second door and was looking up under the seat until his eyes fell on a black case. Pistol reached under the seat while Penny was staring down at him and pulled the black case from under the seat.

"This shit kinda heavy. What the fuck in here?" Pistol spoke to no one in particular.

"Bruh, we got company. Who the fuck them, niggas?" Penny asked peeping the small crowd of niggas jeweled down with bottles of liquor in each of their hands and a stripper a piece.

"Oh shit," Rude said as one of the dudes dropped the bottle looking in their direction.

The dude shouted, "What the fuck y'all niggas doing in my shit?"

Immediately the blood started pumping in Rude's chest as he pointed the pistol at the small entourage and said, "Y'all fuck niggas already know what's up. Get the fuck on the ground."

A big, burly black dude with long dreads laughed. He was clearly intoxicated as he held the chain around his neck, showing the diamonds sparkling even in the darkness then said, "Y'all lil' niggas must wanna die? Nigga we the Last Mafia!"

Boom!

The shot blew half of the big man's face off which caused Rude to look back and see where the shot came from.

Penny stood behind him, the barrel of the pistol smoking. "N'all nigga you must wanna die? Y'all hoe ass niggas get on the ground," Pennywise stated with ice in his words.

The small entourage shaken by the sudden death of their comrade, dropped to the ground, pulling the crying strippers down with them ready to sacrifice the hoes if it came to it. Pistol and Penny immediately converged on the group and began snatching chains, rings, and money out of their pockets. One dude mumbled something, and Pistol stomped his head into the ground so hard with a black Timberland boot that it knocked the man unconscious.

"What the fuck going on out here?" a security guard shouted.

Boom! Boom! Boom!

Rude let shots ring out toward the guard who dived out of the way scampering behind a now bullet filled Mercedes Benz coupe.

"Let's go!" Pistol shouted, eyeing the security guards spill out of the night club.

The three turned, raced back toward the Challenger, hopped in and murked out of the parking lot, fishtailing onto Forsyth Street. Rude didn't see the patrol cars sitting at the light, by the time he did it was too late as the patrol car had already hit the sirens. Rude floored the Challenger and made two swift turns, but they still hadn't shaken the cruiser.

Pistol shouted from the back, "Let me out!"

Rude replied, "Fuck no!"

Pistol said, "I got this, bruh, trust me!"

Rude was reluctant, but he finally pulled over and stopped in the middle of the street. Immediately Pistol hopped out with the F&N Hand Chopper clutched in his hand that he'd gotten out of the black case he found under the seat of the Denali truck. Pistol began running toward the cruiser, firing shots.

Tat! Tat! Tat!

The officer swerved onto a sidewalk and hit a fire hydrant that caused the cruiser to flip over. Pedestrians began to scatter as Pistol let a valley of shots off in their direction.

'*Sweet,*' Pistol thought and ran back toward the Challenger then hopped in to see shocked faces. "This mu'fucka hot," he said with the Hand Chopper across his chest and a wicked smile on his face.

****

Rude, Pistol and Pennywise stepped off the Marta bus in front of the Fulton County Police station on Stone Wall Tell Road.

"Look, baby, just come get me in about thirty minutes. I'm 'bout to hit Moe spot and drop her off some money—I love you, too! Why you keep tripping 'bout what them people saying on the news? They can't tie that shit back to me—as long as you called the rental place I'm straight. Besides I'm not gonna be over there when twelve pull up—a'ight just be here in thirty—love you, too, bye." Rude ended the call and put the phone back in the pocket of his black Adidas pants.

"Bruh, the only thing I'on like 'bout coming over here is we gotta walk right past the police. That shit don't feel right. Plus, we strapped," Penny stated looking at the precinct as they passed it seeing officers standing around congregating.

"Fuck the police, I ain't going to prison," Pistol said, tightening the grip on the chopper in his hoodie pocket.

"Y'all niggas chill. Them folks ain't sweating us. The best place to hide from them hoes is right in they face," Rude stated as he stepped over a fallen tree branch on the sidewalk.

The three turned in the New Landings subdivision, walked through a cut down a hill and came out behind Moe's house. Her next-door neighbor's dog barked at them loudly.

"Shut the fuck up!" Penny said running toward the dog and kicking at it. The dog ran away whimpering.

"Bruh, leave them folk's dog alone, we already hot," Pistol said before the back door opened revealing Moe's four-year-old daughter, Whitney.

"What you doing answering the door?" Rude asked, picking Whitney up in his arms as he headed into the house with Pistol and Penny trailing behind him,

Moe, Bozo, and Wise-Guy were sitting down on the floor of the vacant living room smoking a blunt.

"Fuck going on in here? Where your furniture at Moe?" Rude asked, wondering what happened to her living room set.

Moe looked at Rude with red, glazed, saddened eyes and simply said, "They took it. That's what happens when you can't pay on shit." Then she accepted the blunt from Bozo who leaned back onto the carpet and resumed staring at the ceiling.

Rude looked around the house and saw that it was in disarray and knew that the loss of her things was really taking a toll on the one positive, energetic, and likable woman Rude knew her to be.

Rude decided then to help her out more than he should. He put Whitney down, then turned to Penny who was watching roaches run across a counter. Rude walked up to him and asked for the black bag Penny had in his hands that had everything they had struck for in it. Rude emptied the bag on the small coffee table in the kitchen and bundles of money, jewelry, and what looked like 7 grams of weed fell out the bag. Pistol immediately started popping the rubber bands off the money as Penny reached for the jewelry and started examining it.

Rude picked up the small bundle of weed, sniffed it off drop knowing that it was that pack and threw it across the room. It landed in front of Wise-Guy, causing him to look up.

Rude said, "Roll up." Then he pulled out his phone and ordered some pizza.

"Fuck y'all niggas did hit the bank?" Moe asked with her eyes glued to the impressive mound of money Pistol and Penny were counting.

"Something like that," Rude replied with a smirk on his face.

"Rude we got about twenty thousand, right here. Plus, the jewelry, which we gonna have to find out about. What you want to do about these?" Pistol held up the five different clown masks that were the last thing to fall out of the bag.

"I'on know? Maybe we can use them as masks when we hit our licks instead of them hot ass ski masks," Rude stated grabbing a fist full of hundreds, walking over to Moe and dropping them in front of her.

"What's this for?" Moe asked as she rolled a blunt of the weed Rude had given them to roll.

"It's for keeping shit real with a nigga when I ain't have shit. That's loyalty to me, in my book loyalty is rewarded with loyalty."

"Thank you, baby," Moe said as she stood, then gave Rude a motherly hug and kiss on the cheek.

"I just ordered some pizza. That shit should be here in a minute," Rude said liking to see Moe smile.

It was something he rarely did since the death of Rod and now his mother. Rude knew he had to keep a somewhat clear head and a positive mind-state because the pen or the cemetery was no place for him. So, he welcomed the positive energy he felt off of Moe. Being able to put a smile on her face made him feel like it washed away a million of the fucked up things he had done in the streets. Rude walked over to Bozo and Wise-Guy and gave them both a brotherly handshake.

He took a seat on the carpet with his back to the wall and said, "I see y'all niggas been holding it out down and staying the fuck out the way."

Bozo shook his head and Wise said, "Had to, you know them folks been crawling around here tryna get people to tell something about that bitch ass nigga, Dubb."

"Man fuck that nigga and we ain't gotta speak on that no more that nigga is dead," promised Rude before spotting a rolled up blunt on the carpet

Rude picked one of the blunts off the carpet and yelled at Pennywise who was in a heated debate with Pistol over what mask would be his and threw the blunt. Pistol snatched it out of the air right before Pennywise caught it which started another debate about whose turn it was to light up first. Rude smiled at them, then introduced them to Bozo and Wise-Guy.

"The big one named, Pistol, shawty from the Eastside. The lil' one named, Pennywise, shawty from New Orleans." Rude pulled the blunt, then said, "Bruh, we out to get a check, nothing else. You already know we on the fuck shit but amongst ourselves we all for loyalty. To be given loyalty is to have protection and become the protector of your brother," Rude stated sincerely through a haze of smoke.

Silence filled the air before Bozo said, "You know, bruh, I don' witnessed a lot of bullshit go on in the streets. And a lot of bullshit don' happened to me, but not once, can I truly say I been given my loyalty to a cause. I always thought I could get it myself. I guess that's where I keep coming up short."

"Bruh, I don' did a lot of fuck shit. I'm not gon' lie and sit here looking back on that shit. I can honestly say that shit wasn't worth it, but it's all I've ever been taught. Ever since I was little, all I've ever seen was destruction and pain. Not once have I been accepted for who I really am. That shit turned me into who the streets wanted me to be. But I'on got no family like that, the streets embraced me wholeheartedly and they're all I know. *But I'm tired of being broke, I want it,*" Wise-Guy said adding emphasis to his last words.

"Me too," Pistol agreed, flipping through the thick stack of bills in his hand.

"Bruh, you already know I'm down for whatever," Bozo added, accepting the blunt Penny had just handed him.

Pennywise threw the remainder of the clown masks on the floor at Rude's feet. Rude picked one up and said, "You know a clown is a rude motherfucker. He don't care 'bout shit and always gets the last laugh. That's that fuck shit I be talking about. I'ma win, fuck losing. It's the fuck shit to the end with me. So, what the fuck y'all niggas gon' do?" Rude looked around through the haze of smoke at Bozo and

Wise who had their attention focused on the crazy looking ass clown masks on the floor.

Bozo was the first one to get up, pick up one of the masks and say, "You already know, I'm with the movement." He clasped Rude's hand into his and turned, then repeated the process with Pistol and Pennywise.

"Loyalty, huh?" Wise-Guy said pulling the blunt deeply as his mind raced.

"Till the fuckin' end of time!" Pistol said.

"There isn't enough of this to turn me into a hoe nigga," Pennywise said, holding up a thick stack of money.

Rude threw Wise-Guy one of the last remaining masks and said, "You the last one left. So, what you gon' do? We got shit we need to get established."

Wise-Guy looked down at the mask in his hands and thought about his dead brother, Kid. Then thought about all he had been going through in the streets. How he had been playing around risking his life for crumbs when he could've been had a sack.

"Bruh, I'm all in, but I'on wanna do no petty shit. If we gon' play, we might as well play to win," Wise-Guy said with no hint of sarcasm in his voice.

"Nigga, you think we playing? A nigga just died behind this shit. It's all or nothing with us. We ain't sparing shit!" Pennywise stated, throwing the stack of money on the floor to emphasize his point.

"Bruh, we gotta get our arsenal up," Bozo advised a plan brewing in his head.

"I already know a spot we can hit off Roosevelt—a pawn shop in Fairburn. That shit strapped with vests and everything," Wise-Guy added already plotting the store, but without a team, he was forced to put the move on the back burner.

"Shit, we gon' get that motherfucka, but tonight we gon' celebrate. We officially a family who on the fuck shit," Rude announced feeling happiness flow through his body knowing if Rod was there, he would have been proud.

Moe walked back into the living room with a bottle of liquor, some red plastic cups in her hand and asked, "Who gon' get drunk with me?" She took a seat next to Rude and accepted the blunt Bozo passed to her.

"Shit, you right on time," Wise-Guy said taking the wrapper off the bottle of Absolut and pouring a cup for everyone.

"Fuck shit!" Pennywise shouted, holding his cup in the air.

"Fuck shit," Bozo added, laughing at the expression on Moe's face from the words everybody had shouted holding up their liquor cups.

"*Fuck shit*?" Moe asked, with a quizzical expression plastered on her face,

"Yeah, a new chapter," Rude said before downing the cup of strong white liquor. Rude then laid back on the carpet, put his hands behind his head and thought about the loose strings that he had to tie up, Kissy Pooh and Stacey.

Blakk Diamond

Chapter 10

"Girl, which one of them LMF nigga's you fuck with?" Tameka asked as Rude sat between her thighs getting his dreads retwisted.

Gucci Mane's new mixtape played from the stereo in the spacious living room of Tameka's apartment. Rude blew smoke out of his mouth as he thought about the LMF that had just been mentioned, knowing they had just hit some of them suckers months ago in Magic City's parking lot. A caper he would never forget, especially the stunt Pistol pulled that insured their getaway. "Gurrl, I fuck with Kay fine ass" stated Tameka's friend on the other line.

"Nicky, I know you ain't talking 'bout Kay from Pittsburgh who baby mama—use to strip at club Pleasures?" Tameka could never come to terms with the type of niggas her friend dated.

Nicky sucked her teeth and added, "Don't worry 'bout all that as long as he dropping good dick in me, I'm good."

Tameka rolled her eyes then giggled and said, "Yo' nasty ass better be careful. You know that nigga supposed to have two bodies in the streets that the police looking for him about—your ass—," Tameka rambled on.

'I know this ain't the fuck nigga who set us up?' Rude thought as a plan started brewing in his head to pay Kay an announced visit.

Rude pulled the blunt deeply again and let the weed relax his mind while he gathered his thoughts. Things had been at a standstill lately. Bozo had gotten locked up for driving with no licenses. Plus, he had some charges in Dekalb for simple battery a case he caught at Club Strokers on a bouncer. So, he was on ice which put a major stop to their plan on the pawn shop that was simply to break into the pawn shop through the back using a couple of sledgehammers to break through the brick wall. Rude had his doubts about the plan, but the crew was restless and wanted action. He would figure something out though because time was money and they were missing too much of it.

Rude hit the blunt one more time before placing it in the ashtray on the coffee table in the front of him, then he placed a hand on Tameka's calves and gave them a gentle skill loving the feel of her soft creamy colored skin.

"Um um, not this time. I'm not about to be up all night doing your hair, Rude. Girl, why you all in my business to know who he is. Look, I'm gone, and you need to take care of yourself. Tell, Kay, I said hi! A'ight, bye bitch!" Tameka said before throwing the phone on the sofa.

"Who the fuck that nigga, Kay is?" Rude asked as he thought about the damage, he wanted to wreck on that nigga life, but he knew if he could cap and procure some funds out the deal then he was all for that.

"He ain't nobody, just some nigga with a lil' bit of money who be fucking with these niggas in the city called the Last Mafia. He from Pittsburgh. I know him through my homegirl Blue who from Pittsburgh also. He used to come through the strip club I worked at and throw a lil money every now and then, but he fucks with the weed real hard."

"Describe him," Rude requested as he closed his eyes searching through his memory for the face in the dark shadows of the night they were set up.

"Shit, he brown-skinned, tall, and got a low haircut. Pretty boy ass nigga. Why?"

"That's the same nigga that set me up to get robbed a while back," Rude revealed as the wheels began to churn in his head on how he was gon' orchestrate his strike on Kay.

"I heard he be on that type shit. That's why I was trying to warn Blue stupid ass, but all she sees is commas. So, I'ma let that hoe be a hoe."

"Well, is she tryna get some money? I can rearrange that because homies gotta get it. If a lil money what it takes, I'll easily come out of the pocket for his head."

"A'ight, I'ma holla at that bitch tomorrow personally and let her know the deal. It ain't like the bitch ain't done this before with her scandalous ass," Tameka said, causing them to both erupt in laughter.

"Also, let her know we need to know some exact spots where he might be keeping his stash. But another note, fuck the check, shawty gotta go. I wanna make this shit as easy as possible. So, this what I want you to do—" Rude started running down a plan that at first Tameka wanted no parts of, but due to the fact she'd promised to be there on whatever level she was needed, she stubbornly accepted.

"I appreciate that," Rude said standing after Tameka had let him know his hair was finished.

"Oh, nigga you gone give that dick up tonight. Got me 'bout to go out there and risk my life. I want some cocaine dick," Tameka stated, indicating that Rude get on the soft with her. Something he had been fucking with off and on due to her for the last past months and something that started out as a booster when they had sex, but gradually elevated to repeat usage. Rude like the high from the good coke Tameka had been giving him. It softened the impact of his reality and also gave him a focus that weed couldn't and it was exhilarating.

"A'ight, gon' head and get that shit. I'm about to fix me a drink," Rude replied walking into the kitchen and opening a bottle of Cîroc.

He got a glass and poured a drink taking it down stiffly, then poured another one before walking back into the living room, over to the stereo and changing the CD to a mixed CD with slow jams on it. The sounds of *Silk, 'There's a meeting in my bedroom,'* filled the air setting the mode. Rude then turned, sat his drink on the coffee table and started stripping down until he was nude.

"Let me help you with that," Tameka said, walking back into the living room butt naked with a small gold box in her hand and lust in her eyes.

Tameka sat the box on the table, bent in front of Rude, dropped to her knees and grabbed the lining of his briefs. Then she pulled them down over his semi-erect dick and leaned in and kissed it softly. Rude stepped out of the briefs as Tameka turned to the small box and opened it revealing a nice amount of cocaine. Using one of the credit cards on the coffee table, Tameka scooted some of the coke onto the card and turned to Rude who was stroking his penis. She took it out of his hand and began expertly sucking while stroking him and balancing the credit card in her other hand.

When Rude's member pointed straight out, Tameka brought the card over to his erect penis and began dumping the powder along the top of his dick to the base of it. She then got on her knees and leaned in while Rude held her hair as she snorted up a little of the coke with her right nostril. Then switched to the left and threw her head back as the coke rushed to her head immediately feeling the effects of the drug. Tameka then dropped back to her knees, placed the tip of Rude's dick in her mouth that still had coke on it and began sucking on it softly.

"Ummm," Rude moaned as he felt the coke numbing his penis.

Rude started slightly stroking Tameka's wet mouth as she juggled his balls moistened by the saliva, she let drip out of her mouth. Tameka deep throated Rude as far as she could, then sucked hard as she pulled back off his dick causing a wet pop to fill the air, as she pulled his penis out of her mouth. Rude pushed Tameka back softly on the carpet and kneeled beside her, then turned to the small gold box, took the credit card off the table, snorted the coke in his right nostril and repeated the process in his left one.

"Ahh," Rude muttered, feeling the inexplicable effect of the drug he was becoming to love.

Rude scooped another small scoop out of the box, then began sprinkling it on top of Tameka's supple breasts as he used one hand to massage her clit, making her shake involuntarily, the coke heightening Rude's touch. Rude sat the credit card down on the table, leaned down and placed his mouth around Tameka's right nipple coated with coke and began sucking on it softly while slipping two fingers in and out her pussy.

"Oooh," Tameka moaned as she reached between Rude's legs with her right hand and started stroking his rock-hard dick. Rude let Tameka's nipple go and made a trail with his tongue until he reached her other nipple, this time sucking so hard Tameka arched her back and let out a loud gasp. "Please let me get that dick," Tameka begged with desperation in her voice.

Rude ignored her, parted her legs a little wider and positioned himself between them, hovering over her. Rude leaned down and kissed Tameka roughly causing her teeth to clink together. Tameka wrapped her legs around Rude's torso and pulled pressing into her wet pussy lips. Tameka's hands ran expertly up and down Rude's back as she was squeezing and massaging, sending shocks up and down his body. Rude leaned into the crook of her neck and started sucking lightly alternating between her neck which caused Tameka to shutter.

"Oooh, baby please!" Tameka begged once again, her pussy pulsating uncontrollably.

Rude leaned up, grabbed his penis which was now oozing with pre-cum and began running it up and down Tameka's slit, while he held one of her legs in the air with her feet in his mouth as he sucked her toes.

"Ahh, ahh!" Tameka moaned, her hands gripping the carpet tightly.

Unable to resist her any longer, Rude guided her into position to be fucked from the front. Once over her Rude spread her legs with both hands and then guided his penis all the way to her pussy lips before pushing in and sinking to the bottom in one smooth motion.

"Oh, shit," Rude muttered as he became enmeshed in Tameka's wetness and tightness.

Rude wanting to get take advantage of the situation so he slowed his stroke down before pulling out. Rude then placed his hands-on Tameka's arms and pulled her off the floor, causing her to wrap her arms around his neck. Standing with Tameka in his arms as she squeezed his dick with her pussy muscles, Rude headed to the kitchen, sat on her the countertop and swiped everything onto the floor in one fluid motion. Rude then leaned in and bit her neck as he began to long stroke Tameka's pussy.

"Yes, that's it. Get this pussy, baby!" Tameka moaned as she squeezed her legs tighter around Rude, pulling him in deeper with every thrust.

Rude slowed down stroking, took Tameka's arms from around his neck and commanded her to lie back slowly. Then he slowly pulled her to the edge of the counter and told Tameka not to worry he had her. When he looked back into her eyes and saw the alarm written all over her face, Rude squeezed Tameka's calves tightly and began to first pound slowly and then faster as he found his rhythm.

Smack! Smack!

"Ahh, don't stop baby, don't stop!" Tameka screamed as she felt Rude touching her bottom.

"Don't worry, I got you. This my pussy!" Rude shouted as he repeatedly slammed into Tameka's sloppy wet pussy causing suction sounds to fill the room. Feeling the pressure mount, Rude pulled Tameka to him and wrapped his arms around her as he continued to pump.

"I'm coming baby!" Tameka screamed as she dug her fingernails into Rude's back and her juices began to flow, coating Rude's dick.

"Argghhh, arrgghhhh!" Rude muttered as his seed shot into Tameka's pussy. Rude bit down on her neck, sucking it softly as sperm squirted out of his dick.

"Damn, baby, you gon' make a nigga fall in love with you," Rude said after he regained his senses.

"I already love you, nigga," Tameka stated sincerely as she stared into Rude's light-brown eyes.

"I know," Rude shot back as he kissed Tameka on the nose.

"Oh, it's not over, nigga. I know you ain't think you was gon' fuck me like this without me giving it back?"

Tameka said before squeezing Rude's dick with her pussy muscles, his dick still hard from the effect of the cocaine.

"Oh, I wasn't planning on stopping anyway. I'm 'bout to get me a son tonight."

"Nigga, please." Tameka giggled actually hoping Rude got her pregnant as he carried her to the master bedroom for round two.

Chapter 11

"Damn, that's fucked up how they knocked Big Tone off. You know, bruh, had just come home from doing twenty years on manslaughter," a light-skinned, skinny dude with big eyes and freckles on his face and gold teeth gleaming said.

"Bruh, you know Sweet D was the cause of that shit. Always wanna hit the booty club up and shit. Them niggas got away with about thirty thousand and some jewelry. One of the niggas who was with the family says one of them niggas was from New Orleans and he could tell the other two was from the city somewhere. Guess what though," a big, fat, black dude said with his dreads hanging over his face.

"What?" the light-skinned dude asked.

"Man, them dumb ass niggas didn't have no masks on, and they were some young ass niggas. That's what made the shit so bad. When Sweet D came back to report the shit to Picasso. Big bruh, was on some shit like he got one-hundred thousand out on each of them niggas head and one-hundred fifty thousand just for some information.

"Whaattt?" the light-skinned dude said with an incredulous expression plastered across his face at the amount of zero's that was just put out there for a reward. This made him wish he was in the position to find out who the fuck made a move like that so he could cash they ass in and hopefully move up the ranks in the LMF.

"Hell, yeah bruh. On some real shit, a nigga gotta be a real dumb ass nigga to try the family. We run the streets, and everybody knows that," the big, black dude boasted as he stood to his feet. "Bruh, let's go make a nacho or something. I'm hungry as fuck," the big, black dude stated.

"Yo' big ass always hungry," the light-skinned dude replied as they walked off to their cell.

Bozo contemplated all he had just heard, and the pieces fell right into place on the jewelry and money he saw Rude, Pistol, and lil' Pennywise with. The shit that bothered him the most was the enormity of the lick they hit and even more who it was on. $100,000 was a lot of money, that shit could put him in a helluva position.

Bozo was sitting in the dayroom of 6-North-400 in Fulton County Jail miserable as a motherfucker because even though the crew had the money to bond him out, his pussy ass judge had denied him bond. What made it worse, he didn't even have no major charge. But how the D.A. made it seem to the judge, a person on the outside would swear he was locked up for murder. Bozo looked up at the television from the third row of benches and his mind replayed the conversation he'd overheard, he let his mind ponder a way he could possibly come up on the reward money without being disloyal. The more he thought about it, he saw there was no way to gain off that shit. So, he thought about a way to play up on the two men who he knew as Luck and Fat Boy, Chris.

Bozo had been locked up on Rice Street with them both a few times and had gained trust from them by taking up a few hits, such as putting niggas on the door and handling beef situations that they paid him for. Plus, Bozo had linked up with Luck's cousin on the streets a few years back and he didn't find out the two were related until a few years later. Besides Luck had already pushed up on him about fucking with LMF, but Bozo turned the offer down because he didn't like the flashy way they carried on and more importantly, how them niggas were getting bird fed at the bottom. He saw the glamour that came with rolling with them bitches, cars, clubs, clothes, and respect in the streets, but he wanted none of that.

The only thing that moved him was the check and the fuck shit. Bozo stood, tired of watching video re-runs and decided to gone head and start his plan he knew it was only a limited amount of time before they released him, and he wanted to be on his shit when the doors swung open.

****

Shouts of wages and betting could be heard in the distance as the drug dealers, robbers, and ordinary street niggas shot dice on the sidewalk under the bright streetlamp of Boulevard. Females stood on the side either with their niggas or catching plays themselves, something everybody from 4th Ward did and that was get money. All type of niggas from all over the city came to Boulevard just to get off bombs of dope, catch licks, or just get plugged in. Everybody wasn't naturally accepted in the way that they hoped and were flexed with fake dope, robbed, or even killed. This was the way of the city and if you weren't on your shit you were gonna fall victim every time.

Pennywise was on the dice and was going out bad after losing $5,000, he was geeking on the dice and was down to his last $2,000.

"Bet two-hundred on ten or four!" his fader shouted who everybody knew as Sweet Fingers from his expertise with the dice in the hood which caused most people to stay out of his way.

Not Pennywise who was shooting for his first time. "A'ight, say no more," a frustrated Penny said before niggas started calling out for a bet. Pennywise dropped $200 all around, then picked up the dice and shook them twice before letting them fly out of his hand. A four and six popped up on the dice.

Sweet Fingers screamed out, "Tighten up lil' nigga! You might as well donate the rest of them crumbs in your pocket." This caused everyone to laugh loudly.

"Nigga you ain't talking 'bout shit, bet five hundred!" Penny shot back heatedly, causing a chorus of "*Oooohs,*" to fill the air.

"What nigga? Five hundred, I dun won from yo' sweet ass ten times. Bet the rest of that lil' money in your hand."

Without words, Penny dropped the rest of the hundreds in his hand onto the floor and called out the amount before picking up the dice.

"Shoot nigga! What the fuck you waitin' on?" Sweet Fingers grinned, causing another round of laughter to erupt from the crowd. Pennywise shook the dice and let them out his hand, the first one landing on 1 and the second spinning—the crowd watched until the dice fell on 6. "I knew this nigga was sweet!" Sweet Fingers shouted, picking up all the money off the ground. Pennywise kicked the dice. "Young nigga you should've stayed on the porch," Sweet Fingers said counting the massive stack of money in his hands as he looked at Pennywise.

'I'ma show him who should've stayed on the porch,' Penny thought turning and running back to his apartment.

Opening his apartment door, he saw his dad slumped in his usual lounge chair with a bottle clutched in his hands watching his favorite show *Sanford and Son.* His father didn't even look up from the TV as Penny walked into the house. Pennywise headed to his room, went under his bed and closed his fingers around a bag. Then pulled it from under the bed and unzipped the bag revealing the F&N

Hand Chopper he had swapped his .9 mm for with Pistol and his clown mask.

Pennywise loaded the clip and then sat it on the bed before changing into all black attire. He picked up the mask and machine gun, then walked past his father again who still had not looked up from the television. Pennywise ran through the cut as fast as he could until he got to the opening by the area the dice game was being held. The crowd had dwindled to about seven niggas. Sweet Fingers was one of them and the loudest one as he continued ranting, waving large stacks of money in his hand around. Pennywise slipped the clown mask on his face, cocked the machine gun back then began a steady pace toward the crowd who was so engrossed in the game that they didn't see him until he let the chopper rip in the air.

Blatt! Blatt! Chaos erupted immediately as people began to scatter.

"Y'all fuck niggas don't move, hit the ground!" Pennywise screamed with menace in his voice.

The first one to speak was Sweet Fingers, "Come on, bruh, here go ten-grand. Gon' head and leave us alone, bruh, we just having a lil' fun."

Pennywise walked to Sweet Fingers and shot him point-blank range in the face causing blood and brain fragments to scatter on niggas who were near him.

"Anybody else got some motherfucking advice?" Pennywise barked.

Silence was the answer, Pennywise then began kicking all the money in a pile and reached into Sweet Fingers pockets pulling out stacks of money and throwing them in a pile also. Then turned and ordered everybody else to empty their pockets. Pennywise instructed one of the dudes who had a backpack on to take it off and empty, then stuff the money in it. Immediately the dude jumped up and did what he was told from the fear of death knowing he had kids and didn't wanna leave them over a few thousand.

Pennywise heard sirens in the air and commanded the dude to hurry. Once he was finished, he snatched the bag and commanded everybody to stand up and run. After that, he turned and ran through the cut with a smile on his face, knowing he had gotten the last motherfucking laugh.

****

"Aaahhh," Wise-Guy moaned as he released his load into the woman that laid under him.

Wise-Guy leaned down and kissed the woman on the head before pulling out of her, then crawled off the sex soiled bed and stood on his feet. Wise-Guy pulled the sperm filled condom off his dick, headed to the bathroom that was connected to the room and flushed it down the toilet before taking a piss. Wise-Guy cleaned himself with a wet soapy rag, then went back out into the bedroom only to find that he had fucked his girlfriend to sleep. He stood there for a while admiring the beautiful curves of her body, the soft features of her face creating the smile that tugged at his heart every time he witnessed it, the woman he had cut all others off for and fallen in love with.

Wise-Guy walked over on the other side of the bed, picked his boxers up and slid them on before grabbing his cell phone and a pre-rolled blunt off the dresser next to the bed. Then he turned and walked out of the room into the dimly lit hallway of the small two-bedroom apartment. He walked to the second bedroom and peeked into the room where his girlfriend's son was and saw that he was sleeping. Lorenzo was not his son, but no one could tell him that. He was the only father figure that the lil' boy ever had since he had been birthed into this world. Wise-Guy always wondered who would leave his girlfriend like her, baby daddy did

She was beautiful, intelligent, strong, and independent. Wise-Guy didn't want to seem pressing, so he never brought the subject up. He just put himself in the place of a man in her life, filling a void he knew would ensure that she remained his forever. Wise-Guy softly closed the door and headed up the remainder of the hallway then stopped once he got in the living room to grab his lighter off the table before heading to the sliding door that led to the balcony of the small apartment. Sliding the door back closed, Wise-Guy padded barefoot to the edge of the rail, stared into the starless black night and became enmeshed in his thoughts of one day making it up out the hood.

'I gotta make it not only for me but for my woman,' Wise-Guy thought before sparking the kush filled blunt and letting his thoughts drift back to the first day when he met the woman who stole his breath away.

"Damn, nigga you gon' buy the whole store ain't you?" Wise-Guy's partner Pee-Wee joked who had a few bags in his hands also from purchases at other stores in the South Lake Mall.

Wise-Guy and Pee-Wee had just struck for a couple thousand from a home invasion they pulled earlier that day. They were at the mall buying clothes preparing for Club Crucial where Young Dro was supposed to be making a guest appearance.

"Nigga shut up. I just want my shit to be right you know how I am about this fashion shit. Fly guy til' the end," Wise-Guy said bursting with pride as he picked yet another outfit.

Wise-Guy picked one more pair of shoes in which the store salesman who Pee-Wee had been flirting with continuously ran off to get. Then they headed to the counter where Wise-Guy's eyes fell on the most mesmerizing face he had ever seen on a woman. The light-skinned, hazel brown eyes, the deep dimples in her face that highlighted her mega-watt smile, the feminine way she handled the clothes she was ringing up and feeling he felt just watching her was enough to make him squirm at her sight. Wise-Guy and Pee-Wee pulled up behind a customer in front of them. Pee-Wee was saying something, but Wise was trapped in another realm as his eyes scanned the cashier's face and frame.

'And she got a fat ass,' Wise thought watching the beautiful woman turn around and reach for a hat on the shelf of the DTLR clothing store.

After the customer finished Wise moved up and dropped his items on the counter, never taking his eyes off the cashier's whose eyes were now locked into his.

"How are you doing, Sir?" the lady behind the register asked with a voice soft enough to break even the coldest niggas down.

"You alright, Sir?" the lady asked once again this time a smile on her face.

Pee-Wee elbowed Wise in the side and said, "Please excuse my brother he has a tendency to stare at the beautiful things in life." He smiled flashing a mouth full of gold teeth before turning to the saleswoman who had a tie-dye mohawk hairstyle and resumed their conversation about hooking up.

"Oh, my bad. I ain't gon' lie, I was awestruck by your beauty," Wise spoke before reaching in his pocket and pulling out a large bankroll filled with 2s, 50s, and 100s

that caused the cashier's eyes to widen in surprise. Not one to miss a beat Wise-Guy began flipping through the money piling out two crisped hundred-dollar bills and placing them on the counter asking, "Is that enough?" While staring into her eyes knowing she was infatuated with the bankroll.

"I'on know let me ring this up for you," the cashier answered whose name tag read: Walker.

"So, what you do? I see you got money and that's something I need. This job right here ain't gon' cut it," the cashier said out of nowhere, shocking Wise-Guy again out of his day-dreaming relapse.

"Shit, I do all different kinds of work. Mostly freelancing, but I can plug you into a few people," Wise-Guy lied but just wanting to seem bigger than he actually was so he could step into the woman's life.

"Boy stop lying, I know a street nigga when I see one." The cashier giggled as she rung up the last item.

"Ah, so you not from Roswell then? I thought you might have been one of the city chicks who think they shit smell like roses," Wise-Guy said getting a smile out of the woman.

"Nah, I'm far from that and your total is two-hundred fifty dollars and fifty-three cents," the cashier said, pulling a string of hair out of her face.

"You know you too beautiful, right?" Wise-Guy asked before saying, "What size shoe you wear? I wanna buy you some of them new Jordan's that just came out."

"My size is five and a half and what is this gonna cost me?" the cashier asked while staring into Wise-Guy's eyes.

"Nothing, but a little time and patience," Wise-Guy replied smoothly as he slid the money for his purchase across the counter and the money for the Jordan's for her. The

cashier only smiled, Wise-Guy knew right then that he had played his cards right.

As he stood there on the balcony puffing on the kush filled blunt, he came to the realization that the day at the mall was by far one of the best days of his young life. He had experienced so much destruction and pain, he had begun to lose all sense of love until he laid his eyes on the cashier that day. Wise-Guy turned his head at the sound of the balcony door sliding open. His woman stepped out with a silk robe wrapped around her body and her hair wrapped up with a scarf. Wise-Guy could tell she had just gotten out of the shower by the cherry scent permeating from her body. Wise turned, stared back out into the distance and felt his woman's arms wrap around his waist and her head lay on his bare back. Wise finished off the blunt, flicked it over the rail and turned slowly until he was facing his woman and then wrapped his hands around her waist.

"Stacey, you know I love you, right?" Wise said. "And I will always be there for you."

Stacey looked in his eyes and said, "I know, I love you, too." She stepped on her tiptoes giving him a kiss.

They both stood on the balcony until the sky began to lighten letting the world know it was the beginning of a new day.

****

Stanley Norman was a retired Navy seal whose passion was collecting guns. Through the years he had accumulated an impressive amount ranging from semi-automatics, shotguns, to automatics and even other items that weren't permissible to have, but due to his connections in the underworld of ex-soldiers he had it all. Stanley retired from the

Navy with an honorable discharge after his leg had been blown off in a top-secret mission overseas, so he settled with his wife of ten years and his two daughters in a nice suburban area of Fairburn, Georgia the hometown he was born in.

Stanley pressured by his wife's insecurity and fear of the guns had opened a gun shop named American Muscle on the busiest street in Fairburn, Roosevelt Road. He was reluctant at first, then the funds from the black market started rolling. He knew he couldn't hold them at the house, so the gun shop became his little heaven. It was closing hour and Stanley was ready to get home to Katelyn, his wife who had called him earlier to let him know she was making his favorite dish, chili and beans. Stanley turned the key in the lock, then pulled it out and shook the door. Before turning out and damn near dropping his carry-on on the ground he saw a man a few feet away from him with a hideous clown mask on his face. The man with the clown mask raised his arm and pointed across the street toward a black 2001 Ford Expedition.

Stanley followed his gaze, his eyes fell on the Expedition and he saw shapes of people in the car and then his phone immediately rang snatching his attention from the truck. Stanley then pulled out his phone immediately seeing his wife's face on the screen which caused his heart to speed up with intensity. Stanley pressed talk and raised the phone up to his ear already feeling before he heard her voice what had happened.

"Baby please give them what they want. They have Andy and Kimberly in the truck over here," his wife said which caused Stanley to look at the truck again.

This time the lights were on and he could see his two daughters duct taped in the back seat, hair in disarray and their eyes on him. His wife was in the front seat with the muzzle of a pistol pushed to her head as she held the phone to her face.

Stanley dropped his head and said. "Okay, darling, but put the fucking monster on the phone!" Stanley watched as his wife said something to the man with the clown mask on.

He took the phone and place duct tape back on her mouth then he heard his voice, "Fuck nigga I'on wanna do no talking!" The lights went out in the truck then it pulled off.

"Look you, son of a bitch, I'm gonna cooperate. But if you harm one hair on my family, I will hunt you down," Stanley growled into the phone with fear and anger coursing through his body.

Laughter was the only response before the kidnapper ended the call. Stanley looked up and saw that there were now three men with clown masks on their faces and pistols drawn. He turned to unlock the door of the store in defeat. The shortest one began to bark orders as they pushed into the store up under the moonlight filled sky. Once they were in the store Stanley was immediately shoved to the ground, tied up, duct taped and dragged to the back of the store into his office where a safe was spotted. The short robber ripped the tape off his mouth and asked for the combination. Without hesitation Stanley quickly obliged giving up the code. The robber then began turning the dial on the sophisticated safe, but after the safe cleared the code it asked for a fingerprint.

The robber looked at Stanley and thought what the fuck he got in here, then pointed the Hand Chopper at Stanley and commanded him to stand on his feet. Stanley couldn't so the robber called out loudly for one of his partners who were busy loading guns, rifles, vests, and bullets on the bed of a truck parked behind the building alley.

The big one popped back up in the office and asked what was wrong. The short one explained the situation and without a word, he turned, yanked Stanley to his feet, unwrapped his hands and stood back as he pressed his thumb into a pad on the safe. The door of the safe clicked open and the small robber told the big one to tie Stanley back up. After that, he punched him in the face which knocked him back down, but this time unconscious. The short robber smiled at the big robber's antics, then focused on the safe.

Opening the safe, the robber's eyes fell on four odd shaped objects that clearly resembled grenades. He then picked them up and automatically knew from the weight that they were the real deal, then his eyes fell on rows of stacks of money and jewelry. He turned and grabbed a black bookbag that sat on the ground beside the desk in the office and began stuffing the money in first, then the jewelry and last the four grenades, carefully leaving the miscellaneous paperwork in the safe.

'*Oh, shit we don' struck big,*' the robber thought sitting on the desk, then commenced to watch Stanley until his partners let him know they had loaded as much as they could in the back of the pick-up truck.

After an hour and a half, the big robber came back in the room and let the short one know they had cleared the place out. By now, Stanley had accepted the reality and was no longer worried about the guns because most of them were insured, his mind drifted to his family something that couldn't be replaced if death took them,

"We appreciate it old man." The short robber laughed as he backed out of the office, headed out the door into the night and hopped onto the back of the truck, then dialed

Rude to let him know the mission had been completed and he had a surprise for him.

****

Music blared from the boom box on the dresser of the Motel 8, a stripper party went into full drive as the men of the Last Mafia Family threw hundreds at the three women who were twerking and popping to the sounds of *Juicy J's 'Bands a Make Her Dance'.*

"Bruh, this shit going down in this motherfucker," Dizzy stated throwing money in the air on top of a stripper who had just hit a split and was making her ass bounce up and down with the rhythm of the crazy beat.

There were only five members of the family that Kay had invited to his birthday party. Not wanting to go to the strip club. Just last week one of his closest partners had been roped off by the feds. He had to fall back because once the feds had you, they had you and it was either do your time or become a rat. Kay wanted no parts of either, so when Blue presented the idea of a private party with some of the elite strippers, she knew he accepted it.

Kay had risen in the streets through finesse, cutthroat shit, and pure hustle. This had gotten him scouted and brought into the fold of the Last Mafia. Kay obliged happily knowing his status in the streets would blow up just as much as his check would, so it was a no-brainer when the officer fell in his lap. He had been with the family now for a year and had proven his worth by how he clocked in on the check and how he gained blocks overthrowing niggas he used to fuck with having no regard for past relationships. Only the strong survive was the motto and something he lived by, but the longer his check got the lesser he trusted.

Tonight, even though it was his birthday he felt something in the midst, but he didn't want to ruin his birthday, so he put his gut instinct to the side and relaxed trying to enjoy the night.

Kay tilted the Ace of Champagne back and took a deep gulp before hitting the fat blunt between the fingers of his left hand.

"Bruh, that hoe Tameka going ape shit? I thought she had stopped dancing?" Dizzy said pulling on a blunt of his own.

Kay turned his attention to Tameka who he had been making eye contact with since the party started. Kay made up his mind as soon as he saw she was one of the dancers that he was gon' fuck her. Something Blue had promised him he could get for his birthday her present to him.

"I thought shawty had stopped dancing, too. I know I'm 'bout to get some of that pussy tonight," Kay stated pulling on the blunt deeply again as he watched Tameka clap her ass cheeks together which caused an uproar as his brothers let more money rain out of the sky on top of the strippers.

"I know that's right, bruh, I want next." Drizzy giggled watching Tameka stealing the show from the other girls.

Kay stood, put the blunt in his mouth and straightened his Glock 19 in his tan Armani slacks before he stumbled toward Blue who was fixing herself a drink. Kay looked at Blue's ass from the back and how it swallowed the canary yellow G-string she had on. Kay knew tonight he was going to fuck her stupid.

Kay wrapped his arms around her and pressed his semi-erect dick into her back then said into her ear, "I want, Tameka so come on so I can get my present." Then he groped her bare breast in his left hand.

Blue leaned her head back and moaned, "Okay." Her hand slid behind her giving Kay's penis a gentle squeeze.

Then Blue turned, headed toward Tameka and pulled her by the hand into her bare chest touching. Then whispered in her ear turning to point at Kay and kissing her in the mouth lightly. The two women then turned toward the door adjoining the second room they rented for the strippers to change in and walked through. Kay, ready to play, headed toward the door, walked into the darkened room and was surprised to see two masked men standing in the room.

Immediately he threw the bottle of champagne at the two men and yanked his pistol off his waistline wanting to go out in gun smoke than on his knees.

Boom! Boom! Boom!

To Be Continued…
Fuk Shyt 2
Coming Soon

Submission Guideline

Submit the first three chapters of your completed manuscript to ldpsubmissions@gmail.com, subject line: Your book's title. The manuscript must be in a .doc file and sent as an attachment. Document should be in Times New Roman, double spaced and in size 12 font. Also, provide your synopsis and full contact information. If sending multiple submissions, they must each be in a separate email.

Have a story but no way to send it electronically? You can still submit to LDP/Ca$h Presents. Send in the first three chapters, written or typed, of your completed manuscript to:

LDP: Submissions Dept
Po Box 870494
Mesquite, Tx 75187

DO NOT send original manuscript. Must be a duplicate.

Provide your synopsis and a cover letter containing your full contact information.

Thanks for considering LDP and Ca$h Presents.

Coming Soon from Lock Down Publications/Ca$h Presents

BOW DOWN TO MY GANGSTA

By **Ca$h**

TORN BETWEEN TWO

By **Coffee**

BLOOD STAINS OF A SHOTTA **III**

By **Jamaica**

STEADY MOBBIN **III**

By **Marcellus Allen**

BLOOD OF A BOSS **VI**

By **Askari**

LOYAL TO THE GAME **IV**

LIFE OF SIN **III**

By **T.J. & Jelissa**

A DOPEBOY'S PRAYER **II**

By **Eddie "Wolf" Lee**

IF LOVING YOU IS WRONG… **III**

LOVE ME EVEN WHEN IT HURTS **III**

By **Jelissa**

TRUE SAVAGE **VII**

By **Chris Green**

BLAST FOR ME **III**

DUFFLE BAG CARTEL **IV**

By **Ghost**

ADDICTIED TO THE DRAMA **III**

By **Jamila Mathis**
A HUSTLER'S DECEIT 3
KILL ZONE **II**
BAE BELONGS TO ME III
SOUL OF A MONSTER II
By **Aryanna**
THE COST OF LOYALTY **III**
By **Kweli**
SHE FELL IN LOVE WITH A REAL ONE **II**
By **Tamara Butler**
RENEGADE BOYS **III**
By **Meesha**
CORRUPTED BY A GANGSTA **IV**
By **Destiny Skai**
A GANGSTER'S SYN II
By **J-Blunt**
KING OF NEW YORK V
RISE TO POWER III
COKE KINGS II
By **T.J. Edwards**
GORILLAZ IN THE BAY III
De'Kari
THE STREETS ARE CALLING II
Duquie Wilson
KINGPIN KILLAZ IV
STREET KINGS 2
PAID IN BLOOD 2

Hood Rich
SINS OF A HUSTLA II
ASAD
TRIGGADALE II
Elijah R. Freeman
MARRIED TO A BOSS III
By Destiny Skai & Chris Green
KINGS OF THE GAME III
Playa Ray
SLAUGHTER GANG II
By Willie Slaughter
THE HEART OF A SAVAGE II
By Jibril Williams
FUK SHYT II
By Blakk Diamond

<u>Available Now</u>
<u>RESTRAINING ORDER **I & II**</u>
By **CA$H & Coffee**
<u>LOVE KNOWS NO BOUNDARIES **I II & III**</u>
By **Coffee**
<u>RAISED AS A GOON I, II, III & IV</u>
<u>BRED BY THE SLUMS I, II, III</u>
<u>BLAST FOR ME I & II</u>
<u>ROTTEN TO THE CORE I III</u>

A BRONX TALE I, II, III

DUFFEL BAG CARTEL I II III

By **Ghost**

LAY IT DOWN **I & II**

LAST OF A DYING BREED

BLOOD STAINS OF A SHOTTA I & II

By **Jamaica**

LOYAL TO THE GAME

LOYAL TO THE GAME II

LOYAL TO THE GAME III

LIFE OF SIN I, II

By **TJ & Jelissa**

BLOODY COMMAS I & II

SKI MASK CARTEL I II & III

KING OF NEW YORK I II,III IV

RISE TO POWER I II

COKE KINGS

By **T.J. Edwards**

IF LOVING HIM IS WRONG…I & II

LOVE ME EVEN WHEN IT HURTS I II

By **Jelissa**

WHEN THE STREETS CLAP BACK I & II III

By **Jibril Williams**

A DISTINGUISHED THUG STOLE MY HEART I II & III

LOVE SHOULDN'T HURT I II III IV

RENEGADE BOYS I & II

By **Meesha**

A GANGSTER'S CODE I &, II III

A GANGSTER'S SYN

By J-Blunt

PUSH IT TO THE LIMIT

By **Bre' Hayes**

BLOOD OF A BOSS **I, II, III, IV, V**

By **Askari**

THE STREETS BLEED MURDER **I, II & III**

THE HEART OF A GANGSTA I II& III

By **Jerry Jackson**

CUM FOR ME

CUM FOR ME 2

CUM FOR ME 3

CUM FOR ME 4

An **LDP Erotica Collaboration**

BRIDE OF A HUSTLA **I II & II**

THE FETTI GIRLS **I, II& III**

CORRUPTED BY A GANGSTA I, II & III

By **Destiny Skai**

WHEN A GOOD GIRL GOES BAD

By **Adrienne**

THE COST OF LOYALTY

By Kweli

A GANGSTER'S REVENGE **I II III & IV**

THE BOSS MAN'S DAUGHTERS

THE BOSS MAN'S DAUGHTERS II

THE BOSSMAN'S DAUGHTERS III

THE BOSSMAN'S DAUGHTERS IV

THE BOSS MAN'S DAUGHTERS **V**

A SAVAGE LOVE **I & II**

BAE BELONGS TO ME I II

A HUSTLER'S DECEIT I, II, III

WHAT BAD BITCHES DO I, II, III

SOUL OF A MONSTER

By **Aryanna**

A KINGPIN'S AMBITON

A KINGPIN'S AMBITION **II**

I MURDER FOR THE DOUGH

By **Ambitious**

TRUE SAVAGE

TRUE SAVAGE II

TRUE SAVAGE **III**

TRUE SAVAGE **IV**

TRUE SAVAGE **V**

TRUE SAVAGE **VI**

By **Chris Green**

A DOPEBOY'S PRAYER

By **Eddie "Wolf" Lee**

THE KING CARTEL **I, II & III**

By **Frank Gresham**

THESE NIGGAS AIN'T LOYAL **I, II & III**

By **Nikki Tee**

GANGSTA SHYT **I II &III**

By **CATO**

THE ULTIMATE BETRAYAL
By **Phoenix**
BOSS'N UP **I , II & III**
By **Royal Nicole**
I LOVE YOU TO DEATH
By Destiny J
I RIDE FOR MY HITTA
I STILL RIDE FOR MY HITTA
By **Misty Holt**
LOVE & CHASIN' PAPER
By **Qay Crockett**
TO DIE IN VAIN
SINS OF A HUSTLA
By **ASAD**
BROOKLYN HUSTLAZ
By **Boogsy Morina**
BROOKLYN ON LOCK I & II
By **Sonovia**
GANGSTA CITY
By **Teddy Duke**
A DRUG KING AND HIS DIAMOND I & II III
A DOPEMAN'S RICHES
HER MAN, MINE'S TOO I, II
CASH MONEY HO'S
By Nicole Goosby
TRAPHOUSE KING **I II & III**
KINGPIN KILLAZ I II III

STREET KINGS
PAID IN BLOOD
By **Hood Rich**
LIPSTICK KILLAH **I, II, III**
CRIME OF PASSION I & II
By **Mimi**
STEADY MOBBN' **I, II, III**
By **Marcellus Allen**
WHO SHOT YA **I, II, III**
Renta
GORILLAZ IN THE BAY **I II**
DE'KARI
TRIGGADALE
Elijah R. Freeman
GOD BLESS THE TRAPPERS I, II, III
THESE SCANDALOUS STREETS I, II, III
FEAR MY GANGSTA I, II, III
THESE STREETS DON'T LOVE NOBODY I, II
BURY ME A G I, II, III, IV, V
A GANGSTA'S EMPIRE I, II, III, IV
Tranay Adams
THE STREETS ARE CALLING
Duquie Wilson
MARRIED TO A BOSS… I II
By Destiny Skai & Chris Green
KINGS OF THE GAME I II
Playa Ray

SLAUGHTER GANG II

By Willie Slaughter

THE HEART OF A SAVAGE

By Jibril Williams

FUK SHYT

By Blakk Diamond

BOOKS BY LDP'S CEO, CA$H

TRUST IN NO MAN
TRUST IN NO MAN 2
TRUST IN NO MAN 3
BONDED BY BLOOD
SHORTY GOT A THUG
THUGS CRY
THUGS CRY 2
THUGS CRY 3
TRUST NO BITCH
TRUST NO BITCH 2
TRUST NO BITCH 3
TIL MY CASKET DROPS
RESTRAINING ORDER
RESTRAINING ORDER 2
IN LOVE WITH A CONVICT

Coming Soon
BONDED BY BLOOD 2
BOW DOWN TO MY GANGSTA

www.ingramcontent.com/pod-product-compliance
Lightning Source LLC
Chambersburg PA
CBHW060426260626
47161CB00005B/1797